THE SQUAW MEN

For the last thirty years, Amos Cardiff and Henry Potter had lived with a band of Indians and renegades in an isolated meadow. Now, things were changing as every year settlers crept closer, forcing the camp farther into the mountains. Trying to hold off the whites was seemingly impossible, but the Indian leader, old Tenkiller, would not listen to reason. If Amos and Henry did not do something, the whole camp would be lost.

THE SQUAW MEN

Lauran Paine

GUNSMOKE

This hardback edition 2004
by BBC Audiobooks Ltd
by arrangement with
Golden West Literary Agency

ISBN 0 7540 8272 5

British Library Cataloguing in Publication Data available.

Printed and bound in Great Britain by
Antony Rowe Ltd., Chippenham, Wiltshire

CONTENTS

CHAPTER 1
The Axe Man

They came up out of the swale with the sun at their backs and sat there, men and horses as still as statues. Behind them were blue-hazed mountains, fully forested and dotted by sawtooth escarpments, veined with ice in places sunlight did not reach.

Ahead lay seemingly endless miles of springtime grass, mostly flat but with infrequent swales and occasional trees. As far as a man could see the country was flat. In springtime when grass heads were as high as a rider's stirrups, every slight breeze made them wave and ripple, resembling the pale green waves of an ocean. In late summer and autumn when the grass was cured, the rippling grass created an impression of tawny tan sea waves curling gently in a pervasive silence.

Southeast was a town called Bent's Siding. The name derived from a labor camp where flatcars had brought loads of steel, ties, tools, and supplies during the construction of the transcontinental railway. It had been a busy, noisy place of alien languages, brawny men, sweat, whiskey, and casualties—under the supervision of a company man named Bent.

All that was gone now. The tracks had been dutifully laid and steamcars crossed the land, billowing streamers of dirty black smoke. Bent's Siding had become a thriving frontier community with a redbrick bank building, a tree-lined wide roadway called Main Street, a fire brigade, a town council, four saloons, a Baptist church with the tallest spire in town,

1

and merchants whose world began and ended at the outskirts of town.

But from the perspective of those who lived a few miles from the town, Bent's Siding was a very small cluster of structures, dwarfed to anthill size by the hugeness of the land.

To the two riders who had emerged from the swale to sit their horses looking westward, Bent's Siding might as well not even have existed. Neither man was young, neither carried a spare ounce of flesh. They were weathered and possessed the canniness, wisdom, and knowledge that comes from a lifetime of surviving hardships here, long before there was a Bent's Siding. Their attire was half settlement, half buffalo camp: stained split-hide hunting shirts and old floppy army-campaign hats, grease-layered from decades of sweat and dust; trousers of coarse blue wool from which the soldier stripes had been torn off; the tall, low-heeled, cowhide boots of drovers.

The man with the cud-filled right cheek leaned on his saddlehorn to expectorate aside and before straightening back wagged his head as he said, "That makes two, Henry. The one over on Coffee Creek—he built among them trees so no one knew he was settling in until he was already there. Now there's this one too."

From a distance it would have been very hard to tell them apart. Neither was particularly tall, both were lean as panthers, graying, pale-eyed, with jaws of iron and mouths like bear traps.

Henry Potter scratched, looked out at the wagon camp, at the big harness horses, at the placidly grazing milk cow, and replied as he watched a distance-dwarfed man come from the far side of the wagon, carrying an axe. "No woman?"

Amos Cardiff sprayed amber again before answering. "Didn't see one, but they don't come out here by themselves to steal land. Usually they got a woman an' maybe young'uns."

Henry sat a long time, silently watching the figure hack at a bleached, stone-hard piece of dead wood. He could see the man swing the axe, but there was a slight delay in the sound because of the distance. The air was clear, so Henry and Amos could see details at about half a mile. Total visibility was well over ten miles.

"The old buck won't like this," Henry said. "Amos?"

"What?"

"You know what's been happening, don't you? Two of 'em out here now, next year six or eight, the year after twenty an' more."

"I know. He's been told." Amos turned to regard his companion. "There's nothing he—or anybody else—can do to stop it, Henry, but you know damned well Tenkiller's never going to change. He made a good fight, has for fifteen years. A lot of the others are gone, but he's still thinkin' like old times, like nothing's changed."

Henry stretched in the saddle, watched the far-off man with the axe, and narrowed his eyelids, which were already perpetually squinted. "It'd be better if we didn't tell Tenkiller, but all that'll happen is someone else'll come out here and see this fellow and carry word back to the old man."

Amos shifted his weight a little. "Or, we could come up behind him," he said, pointing toward the stranger, "crack his skull, set fire to his camp an' wagon, and drive them big horses back up yonder with us."

Henry stood in the stirrups, twisted to peer southeast for a moment, then straightened around and sat down. "They'd see the smoke down yonder at the Siding." He lifted his left hand with the rawhide reins in it. "If we done it at night, they'd see the firelight. Let's just head for home and maybe get some camp meat on the way."

Amos grunted and reined around to follow Henry back down out of sight in the swale, which ran crookedly northwest by southeast and kept the horsemen from sight all the way through the jumbled foothills and up higher, where the timber began.

They unavoidably left unshod-horse tracks, but worried very little about this because they were following a game trail; in a few days wild creatures using the same trail would obliterate their sign.

It was a long ride. They did not try to complete it in one day. In mountainous country the best way to end up on foot was to push horses too hard.

They camped at a five-acre emerald meadow with a cold-water spring on the east side where there had once been a trapper's log cabin. All that remained of the cabin now was a front wall and one side wall—the roof and other sides had collapsed from wet-rot.

They camped close to the spring, ignored the haunted old log hutment, got the horses hobbled and cared for, and came up with a fair meal from their saddlebags. The late-day sun was still shining down in open country, but had been cut off from their green meadow by tall, ancient fir trees, too thick to see around.

They laced black coffee with whiskey, a practice they'd followed for more years than either of them cared to count. They got comfortable, ate mostly in silence, then relaxed by fire heat with the pleats out of their bellies, and talked a little.

Apart from discussing the squatter they'd seen back yonder, they talked about a subject they had been kicking around for several months now. Amos pouched a cud of molasses-cured into his cheek on the side where some teeth were not missing, watched his partner stoke up a foul little use-darkened pipe, and sprawled in the trampled grass, head propped on one arm as he said, "If we hadn't got snowed in . . ."

Henry nodded without letting up on his effort to puff up a good head of smoke. Kinnikinnick lost its fire quicker than pure tobacco.

Amos spat into the fire, and the hissing sound was loud in the silence. He was about to go on, when Henry removed the little pipe to look into its bowl at the redness, and spoke.

"What happened thirty years back just upped and happened. Mostly, them that would have staked us out are dead." Henry puffed again, hard, to keep the bowl glowing before saying more. "It was the snow all right, but there's been plenty of chances to get out since then, an' here we are."

Henry gazed dispassionately at this man who had been part of his life since youth. They rarely argued. In fact, although they used to differ from time to time on many subjects, they now acted and thought pretty much alike.

"The women are gone, Amos. The children went out and ain't come back. We're like we was thirty years ago." Henry nursed his pipe for a moment before continuing. "That damned old man's about all that's left of the old ones. Him an' his woman. Otherwise, there aren't tribesmen any more— they been dilutin' the blood for years. There's hardly a full-blood left up there. An' some of the latecomers are a sorry lot. Drinkin', settin' around loafing."

Amos shifted slightly on the fir-needle carpet and looked across the stone ring. "Henry, you've said it before, we could load up and ride on. Where to? Y'know as well as I do there's no place left where we'd fit in but up yonder. And we're old. Everything's been changing to beat hell the last thirty years, except this country, and now it's commencin' to change too. We've set back where we couldn't see the change, and now, for chrissake, it's overtook us. We're like old Tenkiller."

"Naw. He lives in the past."

"To him the past is present. He don't leave the meadow. He's never been to Bent's Siding. Don't even ride in that direction when he goes out with a huntin' party. It ain't livin' in the past for him, so much as it's just simply that he don't know about the change that's comin', and he won't listen. Today to him is the same as things always has been."

Henry reared up slightly to stoke the fire, then settled

back again. "Next time he goes down along the lower mountains he's goin' to see that settler. An' you know what he'll
do. Just like he does things years back. He'll scorch that camp
and leave the settler's carcass in the ash.

"Why didn't the damned fool settler take up land farther
off? Amos, the time's come. We got to fish or cut bait. If
Tenkiller takes some men an' skulks down there in the dark
and raids that feller, folks in Bent's Siding will see the smoke
and maybe send for the damned army. Or maybe make up a
big posse and start scourin' the mountains. This time it won't
be like it was thirty years ago when folks was scairt to come
into the mountains and there wasn't enough soldiers. This
time they'll keep comin' like hailstones. Maybe they'll haul
the Indians off to a reservation, the ones they don't kill, but
us—you know damned well what they'll do to white men
living with Indians."

Amos scoffed. "You already said they're mostly 'breeds
now."

Henry nodded. "All right. They won't take no one to
reservations then. . . ."

Somewhere off to the northwest a cougar screamed. The
men ignored the lion, but sat up quickly to peer out where a
two-thirds moon shed ghostly light upon their distant horses.
The animals had stopped grazing and were standing like
statues, heads raised, ears pointing in the direction of the
scream. They remained that way for a full ten minutes.
When no additional scream came, they went back to grazing
and the pair of campers got comfortable again. Neither one
commented about this little interlude; almost every day of
their past lives had had at least one such moment.

Amos picked up the conversation where the lion had
interrupted it. "You got an answer, Henry? Should we load
up and ride out?"

Henry lay back, looking straight up. There were a million
stars up there. Someone once told him they were not individual entities, but that rather the night sky was a blanket pulled

across the heavens after nightfall; it had a lot of little holes in it, like moth holes, and those little lights were where whatever was up above the blanket was shining through.

Amos said, "Are you asleep?"

Henry replied after a moment of brief speculation about what it must be like past that old, moth-eaten blanket. He said, "We been up yonder a hell of a long time. We know everybody up there. Your woman an' mine are buried up there."

Amos was rolling some molasses-cured between his hands as he replied, "That means you don't really have your mind made up, no matter what you been saying."

"No. It means if the old man won't listen to reason, then we'd better leave before he brings down a whole regiment of cavalry on the camp. Only first, we got to try. I don't want to see it happen." Henry propped himself up again, looking across the dying little fire. "We got to do everything we can, first."

Amos considered the red coals for a while in silence, then grunted around to kick out of his boots, put aside his rolled-up shellbelt and pistol, remove the ancient hat to vigorously scratch, and roll into his blankets like a cocoon. "You mean talk him into leavin' that settler alone?"

"Yes."

Amos grunted again. "I wouldn't be too hopeful if I was you."

"I'm not."

"Well, Henry, I'm tired, and I got no idea where we're goin' to go . . . Nobody can talk the old man into nothin' that's got to do with something like this . . . good night."

"Good night."

The big cat screamed again, but farther off this time. Both old men sat up in their blankets and cursed, but this time their saddle animals only fidgeted a little.

CHAPTER 2
Tenkiller

Generations ago mountain Indians had established a hunting camp here that, in time, became a permanent village.

In those earlier times residences had been conical homes made of stripped hide. Now, there were no hide houses, only log and mud-wattle cabins set in a beautiful upland meadow of considerable size that had a snow-water creek passing diagonally through it.

It was an old camp. In a man-made clearing hidden at the base of a "black-rock" or obsidian cliff where burials had taken place, there were dozens of scaffolds with mummy bundles atop them, all mutilated by birds, many crumbling to earth among the later earthen burial mounds; tradition had yielded to the customs of white Indians like Amos Cardiff and Henry Potter who, refusing to erect scaffolds when their women died, had dug graves instead.

At one time the village had had about fifty residents, perhaps even more if the evidence of tipi rings could be relied upon. Now, there were no more than thirty-odd bucks, squaws, and pups, of which only two or three families looked like full-bloods.

The cabins were sturdy, chinked tight against bitter winters, and each had a storehouse out back. Grass grew lush all summer, dark green and nourishing. Alfileria grew against the ground, its little lavender flowers spreading in all directions among the grass stalks.

Amos's and Henry's log houses were near each other.

8

When the two men returned, they cared for their animals, hauled saddlery inside to protect it from prowling nocturnal varmints, then walked together to Tenkiller's house. It had a roof of sugar-pine shakes, a spread-eagled black bear skin nailed to the south side of the front wall, and a mountain lion hide on the north side with the doorway between.

Inside, the house was gloomy. There were rarely windows in any of the cabins. Candles burned most of the time. Ovens made of mud-wattle and rock were built into corners. There was only one large room. Bedding was occasionally hidden by hanging blankets, but not in this house. Weapons were held aloft by wooden dowels, as were cooking utensils. The handsome, graying woman who had admitted Amos and Henry left the slab door open to admit daylight. Fawn had a dusky complexion, large sloe eyes, and strong cheekbones. Her eyes looked as midnight black as the braids of hair worn inside weasel skins. Otherwise, although she was not young, she appeared to be ageless. When she smiled, full rows of square teeth shone, white and strong.

She jutted her chin Indian-fashion toward the wide bed where Tenkiller lay sprawled under skins cured with the fur left on, and spoke in throaty English. "Too much talk last night."

Amos and Henry studied the large, rawboned old man. Fawn's gaze remained on them until she said, "You can't talk to him now. Tonight he can talk."

The two men returned to the sunshine.

A burly man named Andrew Mullins was crossing an open place between houses and called over to them. "Didn't happen to get over to that settlement, did you?"

Amos was carving a cud, so Henry answered, "No. Didn't go in that direction."

Mullins hitched at soiled old baggy trousers under his paunch and said, "Directly now, someone's got to. Last night we about dried up the supply of whiskey."

Henry and Amos watched with blank faces as Mullins

walked on. He'd been at the camp for about six years, had taken a wife, and they now had three children. Mullins and his brood ate like horses, and he rarely hunted. He was representative of the village's squaw men. He was lazy, shiftless, a bully and, as Henry had once told Amos, probably had been fleeing from someone when he had ridden into the village on a half-dead horse.

They walked toward the west-side cabins and were intercepted by one of the camp's anomalies, a young woman with jet-black hair, a complexion of burnished copper—and blue eyes. She smiled as she said, "I saw you go over there. Ned said you wouldn't be in there long so I waited. One of his horses is lame."

Henry gestured for her to lead the way. Sun Sister was their niece—Henry's wife and Amos's had been sisters. Sun Sister told them the lame horse had prevented Ned from going out with a hunting party.

Amos spat aside vehemently. Her man had four other horses. He was waiting in fir shade outside, where his sapling corral stood. Ned was a tall, fair, rangy man attired in soft split-hide shirt and britches. He nodded without smiling and led them to a bay horse tethered in the shade. The horse was pointing, standing with one front foot out ahead and his weight on the other leg.

Ned squatted next to Henry as the older man ran a probing hand from the horse's shoulder to the pastern, over the tendon and around the coronary band, and stopped. Henry felt beneath the hair near the hoof and straightened up with wet fingers, pale eyes fixed on Sun Sister's man. "Did you look him over, Ned?"

"No. I figured to this morning. He showed up lame last night."

As Ned stood up, Henry's gaze followed him. "Snakebite," Henry announced. He dried his fingers on his trousers and turned to look at the horse. "Good animal, Ned. For his sake, I hope it wasn't a rattler."

As Henry and Amos were walking down the rear side of the cabins, Henry said bleakly, "What does she see in him?"

Amos smiled smugly. "Same thing your woman saw in you back when she was ripe and you was in your prime."

They had not quite reached their cabins when Tenkiller's woman appeared to tell them her man wanted to see them. She considered their owlish looks and chuckled. "He's drinking coffee. I fixed him a drench."

They followed her back to the old house. Inside, three candles mitigated the gloom. The man seated at the table was large, scarred, older than either Amos or Henry but without a strand of gray in his black hair.

He gestured for them to sit opposite, and the woman brought coffee. After an interval of silence he said, "Bad taste this morning." Behind him the woman's black eyes twinkled, but she remained silent. "Did you bring back meat?"

Amos wagged his head. "Poor hunting on the south slope."

Tenkiller sipped more coffee before speaking again. "Too many hunt down there."

Amos didn't disagree, but he said, "It's never good hunting this time of year, when animals can find feed anyplace."

Henry, who had been silent until now, said, "Tenkiller is right, Amos. Too many hunt down there. From the settlement, more'n likely."

Amos said nothing, but inwardly he sighed because he knew his friend was using the old man's remark as an opener.

The mahogany-colored old man put an obsidian gaze upon Henry. "Plume took four men to Coffee Creek, but they had to come back. That settler who built his cabin in ʾhe trees, like a fort, had a lot of visitors."

"Hunters?" Amos asked.

"Maybe no. Plume thought they were newcomers, maybe settlers. They had horses and cows, wagons and plows on the ground."

Amos leaned back off the old table and met the black stare

of Tenkiller, who said, "You didn't see tracks down there in open country going from the Siding west to Coffee Creek?"

"We didn't go out that far," Amos replied truthfully. "Only down to the last timber."

The old man finished his black coffee and waved the woman away when she came to refill his cup. "We have to know," he told them. "You two can find out. They wouldn't wonder about you being in the mountains."

Henry cleared his throat. The sound made Amos wince. "Yeah, we can find out who they are, Tenkiller, but there's likely to be more to it than that."

When Henry paused, the old man watched him with unblinking eyes. "What more, Henry? No settlers! This is our country!"

Amos and Tenkiller's woman exchanged a quick look before she turned her back and began to busy herself at the hearth.

Henry brought forth his little pipe, but put it away because he knew Tenkiller would not allow it during a palaver. Although Tenkiller had grown up at a missionary school—having been taken there as a small child after soldiers wiped out his village—and knew about the ways of the whites and their language, he had grown up stubbornly wanting the Old Way.

"How many people did Plume see at Coffee Creek?" Henry asked.

"Twelve men, nine women, some children."

Henry pulled down a deep breath and leaned on the table. "Tenkiller, that's too many. They most likely got supplies down at Bent's Siding. Folks will remember them. It's not like going down to burn out one settler."

The Indian sat, looking stonily at the men across the table. They had seen this expression before. He was unyielding.

Henry continued, "I know how you feel. I feel pretty much the same way. We've been together a long time, on lots of hunts and raids together. Tenkiller, a raid at Coffee Creek will bring the army. You know right well what the soldiers will do because you seen it done to your camp years back. There won't be nothin' left but ashes and dead people."

Tenkiller carefully placed his empty cup to one side, planted both arms on the tabletop, and replied. "These mountains go north all the way to Canada. We know them better than settlers or soldiers. No one can find us up here unless we want them to. We can kill them one at a time."

Henry answered cautiously. "That's what I'm saying, Tenkiller." He gestured with an arm. "This is our home. These are our mountains. We don't need plow land. Our families are buried here. Our cabins are here. This is our meadow. If we have to hide from the hunters, they will come here and burn the village, loot the burial scaffolds. If we go, what can we carry except guns and some iron pots, some flour, and coffee? Why would we trade what we have here to burn some settlers, take their horses, and kill their cows, when next year more settlers will take their places? Every year more—down *there*, Tenkiller, but not up here. They couldn't survive up here. They wouldn't even try."

Henry was sweating. The woman was standing with her hips against the wattle hearth, arms crossed, her eyes fixed on Henry.

Several blue-tailed flies buzzed loudly, seeking an opening in the skins draped at the doorway. Flies avoided dark places.

Tenkiller sat hunched and silent for so long it seemed that he might never respond, but eventually he said, "It would be better in Canada. There will never be many settlers up there. The seasons are short for planting and harvesting. The winters are long and cold."

He turned his attention on Amos, who had been quiet. Finally, Tenkiller thrust his chin toward the doorway. His visitors arose and, without another word, walked out into sunlight and resin scent.

As they walked, Amos surprised his friend. "You sounded like Dan'l Webster back there. Sounded good. But you might just as well been talkin' to a tree. Only now he's not going to visit us at night anymore to sit around remembering the old hunts."

Henry strode along, head down. "Like I said down yonder, Amos, we had to try. I didn't figure it would work, but it had to be said. Hell, more settlers down at Coffee Creek . . . if Tenkiller raids down there, whoever comes after us won't let up, Canada or no Canada. What'd he say? Twelve men, children, and nine women? Amos, that would be a goddamn massacre, not just a raid. He'll get everyone killed, sure as I'm standing here!"

CHAPTER 3
An Encounter

Plume was a dark full-blood with coarse features and the physique of a bear. The whites of his eyes were muddy. He sat on a bench in Henry's cabin, relating what he'd seen down at Coffee Creek, and concluded by making a slashing gesture with one powerful arm. "With six men, it can be done by going close on foot, starting fires to see by, and shooting the people when they start to run."

Henry handed the Indian a tin of hot coffee off his wood stove. "And what will happen afterward?" he asked, seating himself on an old bench, feeling warmth in his hands through his metal cup he was holding. "It's not like it was in the old days, Plume. Then, after a raid only buzzards and coyotes came. Now, there's a town full of people. They got singing wires down there—they'll call for the army. Then what will happen?"

Plume drank his coffee, put his cup aside, and smiled at Henry. Tenkiller had already told him about the palaver in his cabin the day before. "Then we do like we've always done. We hide in rocks, in the tall grass, even in burrows. We kill soldiers—one, two, four, or five at a time. Then we disappear again."

Henry leaned back, gazing at the Indian. Plume sat a while longer absorbing the stove heat, before arising and departing.

Henry searched for his bottle, found it at the bottom of a flour sack, took it back to the bench, and was sipping from it when Amos walked in. Before he got clear of the doorway, Henry said, "Crazy people! They ain't learned even yet. Not even after the army took payment for Custer, then settled up for every damned massacre they knew about. Redskins have lost everything and are down to hiding out in the damned mountains, too dumb to understand why. If Plume goes down to Coffee Creek with a band, that's the end of everything for them. And not only for them."

Amos stopped near the stove, considered the agitated face of his old friend, and held out his hand for the bottle. Henry handed it over, shoved out his legs, and sat in evening gloom, staring at his scuffed toes.

Amos handed back the bottle, ran a soiled sleeve across his lips, and said, "Do you think the old man is really sending out a raiding party?"

"Sounds like it. It's plain crazy, Amos. Tenkiller's got everything right here in the meadow. Everything a man his age could want."

Since returning to the meadow neither of them had even thought about the man with the axe. They were preoccupied with the possibility of a massacre down at Coffee Creek and its aftermath.

Perhaps without realizing it, they had lived with tribesmen too long. They now sat as Indians sat. With dusk passing and night approaching, they sat in silence, occasionally passing Henry's bottle back and forth. When it was dark Amos grunted, rose to his feet, and left.

The moon did not appear at the meadow until quite late because it could not penetrate clustering treetops unless it was almost directly overhead.

Henry eventually hid the bottle again and stirred up a small supper fire. Outside, a horse nickered somewhere and was answered from the east, over where the big meadow blended with heavy timber.

He cocked his head, waited, then went back to making a meal. He ate at his scarred, old, uneven four-legged plank table, swilled coffee, then took his utensils out back a dozen yards to the creek and cleaned them, using cold water and silt.

Northward a soundless shadow was moving close to Ned Travis's corral. Henry stood stock-still, watching. It was impossible to discern much, but as he watched the silhouette glide from watery-weak starshine to the darkness of Ned's cabin, he was sure the man was not Sun Sister's husband.

There had always been horse thieves in camp, although they did not steal from other members of the community. Stealing a horse did not mean the same to Indians as it did to settlers and townsmen.

Among redskins, it was a source of pride to be able to steal someone's horse right out from under his nose. It was a coup, a masterful accomplishment. They were honored, not hanged for it.

The longer Henry watched, the more convinced he became that the shadow did not belong to an Indian. Henry had no weapon, only his tin dish and cup, a stag-handled fork, and a cooking pan. But what held him motionless was the suspicion that whoever the horse thief was, he either had to be someone who had come down from the north over icefields and treacherous glass-rock, probably a fugitive, or he had come from the south, the open country of settlers, townsmen, cattlemen, and teamsters.

It had happened before, but rarely. The only outsiders who had found the secret meadow were still there, either part of the community or buried beside it.

The shadow approached from the west. There were trails in that direction, some old, well marked, and traveled. The silhouette halted behind a huge sugar pine where Ned Travis had imbedded an iron stud ring. The man was studying the horses. There were five, and so far the animals had not picked up his scent, which was unusual even on a still night. The stranger turned his head slowly, warily. Henry held his breath, because although he was backgrounded by gloom and large trees, he was still in the man's view. Evidently the man saw nothing that worried him. He leaned a little, seemed to fumble with the tie-down on his holstered sidearm, then crept clear of the sugar pine in the direction of the corral at the precise moment the soaring lopsided moon passed behind a cloud.

Henry could finally move. For seconds he debated whether to return to the cabin for a weapon, or to continue stalking the shadow. He decided to go after the man; it might take too long to get a gun.

By circling out and around, which involved wading across the creek, he got farther away and deeper into the cover of the timber before turning westerly and coming down in the direction of the big sugar pine, the last place he had seen the horse thief—or whatever he was.

Now, finally, Ned's horses were alert. They made no noise. They simply stood motionless, heads high, ears forward, which provided Henry with a line of sight to follow, but he could not locate the man.

A second shadow appeared, tall, lean, and recognizable. Henry let his breath out slowly as he saw Sun Sister's husband. Ned did not seem alarmed as he headed in the direction Henry had last seen the interloper. Henry followed Ned, who eventually met the other man on the northwest side of the corral.

Henry moved to a tree and leaned there, watching in the weak starlight. The men were talking, but no sound reached Henry. Curiosity inclined him to move closer, but he resisted the urge because, while he knew nothing of the stranger, he knew Ned Travis was as skilled a sign reader, tracker, and hunter as anyone at the camp. He had been with hunting parties that included Ned and had been impressed with the younger man's uncanny abilities as a mountaineer. He could detect movement even on a dark night.

They parted, Ned back in the direction of the cabin, the stranger around behind the corral on a southerly course, exactly as he had approached, only now Henry Potter was leaning on a large tree in the oncoming man's path.

Henry turned, moved soundlessly as far as a creek-side blackberry thicket, pushed his way deep into it, and gritting his teeth as thorns dug his hide, crouched.

The stranger passed by about five yards distant, did not slacken his gait or look left or right. He left Henry with the impression he was in a hurry.

A half hour later, when Henry got back to his cabin with the items he'd rinsed at the creek, he lit one candle behind a hanging blanket, sat down and picked out thorns, drank some cold dregs from his dented old coffeepot, bedded down and lay awake until the cold made him burrow deeper. He finally slept.

In the morning he was awakened by children playing on the west side of the camp and several women laughing at the creek, probably filling buckets or washing clothes.

He groped for his hat, boots, shellbelt, and old knee-length coat, and would have gone out back to wash if Amos hadn't appeared, looking worried. "You sick?" Amos asked from the doorway.

Henry scowled. "No."

"You must have put in a long night, Henry. I looked in on you twice this morning and you didn't even stir. You wasn't dead, because you was snoring."

Henry went to the stove, lifted a plate, leaned to blow for coals, found none and went rummaging in the kindling box as he said, "Come in and sit down."

Amos obeyed, watched Henry get the fire started, and waited. When Henry was ready, he told his old friend exactly what he had seen last night.

Amos continued to sit in silence, gazing at Henry for a long while before saying, "Fry your meat, then let's go. As long as whoever he was didn't have wings, he left tracks."

Nothing more was said until Henry had breakfasted. Then he took down his rifle and followed Amos outside into sunshine, around the house in the direction of the creek, and southward so that they would not be seen by the women.

The morning remained cool. There was a high overcast that occasionally covered the sun, and while that did not noticeably change the temperature down in open country, in the forested high country it did.

Amos found the sign. If the man who had left it had had any idea he might be tracked, he certainly would have moved farther from the creek where pine and fir needles rotted rapidly and the ground was spongy.

They had no difficulty. The man had been wearing boots, not moccasins. His imprints were deep enough to make Amos guess he was heavily built.

They eventually came to a place where horse droppings indicated an animal had been tethered among the trees for a considerable length of time. They stopped here for Amos to cheek a cud of molasses-cured and wag his head as he eyed the hoof marks. Henry stuffed his pipe as he eyed them also, and said, "Well now, Mister Cardiff, what we got here to my way of figurin' is a settler or maybe a man from the Siding. Anyway, he rode a shod horse and wore drover's boots."

As usual, Henry could not talk and puff a head of smoke at the same time, so he said no more until the Kinnikinnick was glowing. By then, Amos had walked around a little, examined the ground, and had come back to say, "If we keep on his trail we're going to be way down-country, and you know how I feel about walking, specially in the damned mountains. But I'd like to know if he turned off southeasterly toward the Siding or went in some other direction."

Henry removed the pipe. "Toward Coffee Creek maybe?"

Amos did not answer the question. He was gazing northward. "If we spent a day or so trackin' him, we'd know where he went, and mostly likely where he come from. But them things don't interest me near as much as what he was doin' up yonder and what him and Ned was whispering about in

the middle of the damned night out behind the corral."
Amos paused to turn toward Henry. "Ned could tell us. That
way we wouldn't have all that walkin' and puffing to do."

Henry squatted, sending a unique aroma of pipe smoke
upward and outward in the hushed and breathless forest.
When the pipe finally went out, Henry knocked it empty,
stirred the dottle to be sure there were no coals, then stood
up and hitched at his shellbelt and holstered pistol as he said,
"How do we convince her man he should tell us?" It was
difficult for him to say "Ned Travis." Henry usually called
him "her man" or "Sun Sister's man" because he did not like
the man, even though Ned was the husband of Henry's only
living blood kin.

Amos had no answer. "Let's go back," he muttered, and
struck out, old grimy hide shirt flapping as he walked, slate-
gray eyes squinted in concentration.

It required more time to retrace their tracks than it had to
find the horse sign. To find that, they had walked downhill—
getting back was all uphill, and although there was still no
real heat in the day, hiking in the mountains was sweaty
work.

When they were close enough to the camp meadow to
smell cooking fires, Amos called a halt and went to sit on an
ancient stump, head slightly cocked at his companion. "Tenkiller would have a damned frothin' fit."

Henry spat, then nodded. "Yeah. But no one's going to tell
him until we know more'n we know right now. Amos, I been
figuring on the walk back . . . Whoever that lowlander was,
he come sneakin' in the night and Ned met him the same
way. That's got to mean whatever they're hatching is something the folks on the meadow wouldn't like."

"Such as?"

Henry flared up. "How in hell would I know?"

Amos arose and walked ahead up the trail without another
word. They reached the creek behind the cabins and knelt

to drink, wash, and linger a while, listening to the music of water over stones.

Henry might have talked more, but Amos did as he ordinarily did when he was disinclined to keep a conversation alive: he grunted, got to his feet, and walked off in the direction of his house.

Henry went out to the little shed and pen where he kept his horse, leaned there listening to the horse chewing dry grass—a sound he enjoyed—and was finally going around front to get some soap and a towel from the cabin so he could return to the creek and scrub, when Tenkiller's black-eyed, handsome woman appeared. Fawn looked steadily at Henry for a long time before announcing that her man wanted to talk.

Henry hung fire. The woman, who was erect, sturdy, and wise, said, "Plume is gone," then walked away, leaving Henry staring after her.

Plume had told Henry the night before that he wanted to raid the gathering of settlers down at Coffee Creek. Henry swore fiercely under his breath as he struck out toward Tenkiller's log house.

CHAPTER 4
Trouble!

The old man was hunched at the table, eyes fixed on the open doorway as Henry entered. Tenkiller's expression was sly. He said nothing until Fawn had brought tin cups of coffee, then he spoke.

"They went scouting."

Henry considered the cup. "Yeah," he said softly and dryly before raising his eyes to the old man's face. "I been on scouts with Plume." What he left unsaid was that the scouting party could turn into a raid.

"There's too many of them," Tenkiller said, acknowledging the unspoken, "and they're too close. If there weren't no women they'd just be hunters. With women and big wagons, they come to settle. There's another one—maybe you'n Amos saw him the other day when you was down south. He's got a woman too." Tenkiller sipped coffee, put the cup aside, and leaned forward.

Henry met his stare head-on. "How long we been here?" he asked. "My woman is buried here. We own these mountains. Tenkiller, there's nothing up here they want."

"They'll hunt up here, Henry. Someday they'll come this far."

Those things were probably true, but what was truer was that killing them would bring on a war that the hideouts could not win. Henry drained his cup. There was no easy answer—but there was an answer. "If something happens to their horses, Tenkiller, and if rattlesnakes appear around their camps and wolves howl close at night . . ." Henry noticed Fawn was smiling encouragement from behind her man's back.

Henry fished for his little pipe and stoked it under the steady gaze of the old man. Tenkiller did not use tobacco in any form, but he enjoyed the smell of it. He waited until Henry had puffed up a cloud of smoke before speaking again. "When Plume comes back I'll send him to talk to you."

Fawn turned back to the mud-wattle hearth. Henry considered the red glow in his pipe bowl. Tenkiller had just passed the initiative for ridding the country of settlers to Henry, which meant whatever happened now, he would get the praise or the blame.

He said, "Not if Plume makes a fight down there. It'll be too late."

"He won't start a fight."

"You told him not to?"

Tenkiller nodded his head.

Henry puffed again before commenting. "Plume is Plume. I've known him since he had moss in his pants. When he sees a chance he takes it. I went on his first raid with him. Do you remember that?"

Tenkiller shifted slightly on his bench. "He was younger then. He needed a coup."

Henry smiled bitterly. "Yeah. After that the damned soldiers didn't let up for a solid year. We lost seven men."

"I told him only to scout, see what they were doing down there, to count them, listen to their talk, then come back."

Henry grunted as he got to his feet. "I'll wait for him," he said, signifying that as far as he was concerned, this discussion was ended. But when he was over by the doorway he turned back to say, "Did Sun Sister's man go with him?"

"Yes. Him and Andy Mullins and three others."

Henry left and crossed toward his cabin, streaming smoke from his pipe. The sun was high and the veil-like high overcast that had been noticable several days earlier was gone. There was pleasant, thin warmth.

He ate, napped until late afternoon, then went back to the creek with his buckets for house water and encountered Sun Sister kneeling over a big rock with some wash. She looked up and smiled as she wrung faded cloth nearly dry with powerful hands.

He squatted. "Your man's gone?"

She doused another garment in the creek. "Yes. He left on a scout with Plume and some others."

Henry found a small snow-white pebble and flicked it into the water. "Has he left the camp lately, maybe to scout or hunt?"

"Yes. The day after you and Amos returned he went down below for meat." Sun Sister stopped beating the garment on the rock. "He saw a prime bear but missed it."

Henry flicked another pebble. Ned was a dead shot. Henry had hunted with him many times. He wouldn't miss anything as large as a bear.

Sun Sister kneaded the garment and dunked it again, muscular arms working hard. "Then he went north toward the high country of dirty ice and brought back a fat barren doe."

Henry returned to the cabin with his buckets, set them inside the doorway, and went over to Amos's cabin; it was empty, so he went around back where Amos kept his two horses. One horse was gone. In waning daylight he gazed at the remaining animal, a short-backed, slightly pigeon-toed bay with a mule nose. Amos was probably hunting. It crossed his mind that he might have gone on the scout with Plume, but he doubted that, so he returned to his cabin, lighted two grainy candles, and started a supper fire.

Dusk rarely lasted long at high elevations, especially in heavily timbered country. Henry stoked up the fire to keep chill air outside and patiently waited.

It was a very long wait. He was asleep when someone

rattled his door. It was Amos, wearing an old horseman's coat lined inside with red flannel. Henry lit another candle and watched his friend shed the coat.

As Amos took position with his back to the dying fire, he said, "I followed fresh tracks southwest for a while this morning, then turned up-country to hunt." Amos paused, gazing steadily at his host. "There was two gunshots a long way off and down-country."

Henry shook his old speckled-ware coffeepot, then put it where heat would reach it and stoked up the fire. He said, "Coffee Creek?"

"Maybe. A few more shots and I could have placed 'em. Seemed like it was in that direction. Has Plume come back yet?"

"I haven't see him and he's supposed to come see me when he gets back."

"Why?"

"I told Tenkiller there's ways of gettin' settlers out of the country without lettin' them know we're up here. Steal their horses and scare the whey out of their womenfolk."

Amos went to a bench and sat in silence until he was handed a cup of hot coffee. He blew on it, but it was still too hot so he put it aside. "If it was Plume did that shootin', then those wagon people know someone is up in here somewhere." Amos brought forth a sticky twist and picked lint off it by candlelight before cheeking a cud.

"Tenkiller knows about the axe man. I think he was told by Ned. Sun Sister told me he went hunting down yonder some days back. She said he shot at a bear and missed it. He never missed anythin' as big as a bear since I've known him."

Amos tried the coffee again. "That feller we tracked the other day—maybe the feller you saw skulkin' around in the night and meeting with Ned out back was the axe man."

"You want somethin' to eat?"

"No. I had buck liver about sundown. I got a big one—if you're a little shy of meat, I'll bring you over some . . . Henry, too damned many things goin' on that make me uneasy. What d'you say about ridin' down and talkin' to the axe man?"

"First I want to hear what Plume's got to say. If there was a fight down there, maybe we'd better just keep on ridin' after we see the axe man. I got a bad feeling."

Amos drank half the coffee, put the cup on Henry's big table, and got to his feet. He stretched, picked up the hide coat and, holding it over one shoulder, said, "I'll be out back when you're ready in the morning."

Henry barred the door after Amos's departure, drew off some hot coffee for himself, and blew out two of the candles before sitting down to wait.

It was a good day's ride down to Coffee Creek and a little longer returning because the trail back was all uphill as far as the meadow. If Plume's party returned before dawn Henry would be surprised.

In fact, they had not returned well after sunrise, which caused a little uneasiness in the meadow. Tenkiller came over to Henry's place as expressionless as ever, but clearly troubled.

While they were talking, a ringing high call rode the morning air from the farthest side of the meadow. It sounded faint but clear.

Henry and Tenkiller went outside. There were other people standing like statues, looking westerly, but it was a long while before horsemen broke clear of the dark forest.

They rode bunched up and without haste. Henry got a sinking feeling in his stomach as he stood with Tenkiller. That was the way men rode who were supporting someone on a horse.

Some of the watchers, mostly women, started toward the oncoming riders. Amos appeared from behind his house.

A solitary rider appeared from the eastward timber, unnoticed by the people who were facing the opposite direction.

Amos heard him and turned, watched for a while, then faced forward again. The solitary rider was Ned Travis.

One of the distant men left the others to lope ahead. Tenkiller said, "Plume," and sounded relieved.

Henry watched the muscular warrior scan the little groups until he saw Tenkiller in front of Henry Potter's house. He picked up the gait a little, crossed the wide opening between the cabins on the west side and those to the east, and halted a few yards from Tenkiller. Slackening his reins, he said, "They shot the Mexican."

Tenkiller said nothing as the riders came into camp. The wounded Mexican was helped from his horse; a stranger, also wounded, was lowered to the ground.

The Mexican was an Indian, at least mostly Indian, who had been caught trapping ten years earlier, up beneath the northward glaciers. They called him the Mexican because when they caught him he yelled in Spanish, but he said he was a Pima, from a great mud village hundreds of miles southwest.

"How did they shoot him?" Tenkiller asked.

Plume looked uncomfortable as he slid to the ground beside his horse. "We got down there before daylight, hid the horses, and went ahead until we could see them when daylight came . . . They were everywhere gathering wood, looking after their animals, making fires and talking and—"

"How did they shoot the Mexican!"

"We were lying down hidden by trees . . . There was one behind us. Maybe he went into the timber country in the dark to be ready to hunt when daylight came. We were watching forward . . . He tried to sneak around us, but the Mexican heard him and jumped up to shoot. The settler fired first."

From the middle distance Amos said, "There was two shots."

Plume looked over at the five men approaching on horseback, two of them wounded. "The settler hit the Mexican, but he fired before he fell and hit the settler."

Tenkiller was standing arrow-straight, his wide mouth pulled flat. For several seconds he remained like that, before he brushed past Plume and strode directly toward his house. He kicked the door open and walked in, leaving the door open.

His woman was not there. She was with the other women who had carried the Mexican into his cabin and were caring for him. The second wounded man was put on a bearskin pallet and ignored until Sun Sister arrived. She went to work on him with a basin of water and clean rags.

Outside, Ned Travis walked over to Henry and Amos, watched the activity for a moment, and said, "Hell to pay."

Amos eyed Ned. "You was with them? Why'd you come around into camp from the opposite direction?"

Ned stood gauntly tall, thumbs hooked in his shellbelt as he replied calmly, "Comin' back I rode lower down, watchin' for riders. I figured if they chased us, they'd skirt around the lower country."

The other raiders had dispersed to care for their animals. Tenkiller had not emerged from his house. The sun was high; women and children were apprehensively visible in doorways and passing among the cabins.

Henry started toward the Mexican's cabin. Tenkiller's woman had the Mexican washed and was poulticing a wound in his side when Henry entered the house. Three other women stood close to obey whatever Fawn told them to do.

The Mexican was sweaty, and from time to time he had tremors. His black gaze met Henry's stare and moved away. Tenkiller's woman sent for whiskey and poured half a cupful down the wounded buck.

Henry turned aside, saw Sun Sister, strolled over, and stopped. The other injured man was a stranger. He had reddish-roan hair, thin features, blue eyes, and a stubble of reddish whiskers. He looked straight at Henry until Sun Sister shifted position, cutting off his view.

Henry returned to the sunlight.

Amos accepted what his friend had to say with equanimity. "Better they fetched him back than that they left him down there to tell the others he come onto a party of warwhoops lyin' in the underbrush, spying."

Henry tipped whiskey into their tin cups. "They'll hunt for him, Amos. When he don't come back to their camp they'll start lookin', and if they got just one of 'em that can read sign—"

"Not very hard, they won't," Amos interrupted to say as he raised his cup. "I've yet to see a settler in his right mind who'd go chargin' into the mountains to find someone. Especially after they heard gunshots."

Henry put the bottle back into his flour sack, sat down, and watched the activity across the opening from his doorway. "Worse yet. They'll make a beeline for Bent's Siding."

Amos drank deeply, blew out a ragged breath, and said nothing more.

CHAPTER 5
David Law

By the time things were more or less back to normal it was too late for Henry and Amos to leave. The sun was high, and the big meadow was alive with wild bees and other flying insects. Except for the silence, it might have been just another day.

Although children made noise, the adults went about their business in silence. No hunters left the village. Some men gathered at the corrals behind the cabins to talk quietly. The feeling was that Plume had been reckless. A couple of men who had ridden with him were defensive, but the obvious fact was that he had not scouted adequately or he would have found the settler before the settler saw them.

Tenkiller was angry and summoned Plume to upbraid him. He told Plume what Henry had said about his irresponsibility; when Plume was finally dismissed and passed Henry, Plume refused to even look at him.

There were other angry people in the camp. They'd had time to speculate, and now they did not like the idea of a white-hided stranger being in the camp; any way a person looked at it, the wounded settler, or whatever he was, meant trouble.

Sun Sister told Amos the man's wound was not serious but that he had lost a lot of blood. The Mexican's bullet had passed through the man's upper leg, making a ragged hole where it exited. He was weak, but the wound itself would heal in time; the leg bone had not been hit.

Amos said dryly, "Unless it gets infected," to which Sun Sister replied, "I don't think it will. I washed it all the way through with medicine and plugged it with salt."

Amos went to the Mexican's cabin. The stranger was awake, but the Mexican was sleeping like a bear. When Amos squatted beside the stranger's pallet the man looked hard at him, then said softly, "You're white."

Amos ignored that. "How do you feel?"

"Like a goddamn Indian shot me."

Amos nodded. "I expect you lost a lot of blood. You feel weak and light-headed?"

"Weak as a kitten in a box of shavings, mister. That woman who patched me up put salt in the wound. You ever have that happen?"

Amos smiled as he nodded his head. "Burns like a son of a bitch, don't it?"

The stranger did not reply. He lay perfectly still, studying Amos. After a long while he asked, "Where is this place?"

"In the high mountains. Who are you? What's your name, and what are those folks down yonder doin' here?"

The man raised a filthy sleeve to push sweat off his face before answering. "My name is David Law. I came out with those people to see about settling." David Law's eyes did not leave Amos's face, even when Tenkiller's woman entered to kneel beside the Mexican. "Is this an Indian camp?" he asked.

Amos settled more comfortably before answering. "Well, there's a few full-bloods. Not many. Mostly they're 'breeds of one kind or another, with a few whites mixed in. That man who shot you is called the Mexican. He's part Indian, part Mex."

David Law's gaze drifted over to where Tenkiller's woman was washing sweat off the Mexican, who did not awaken. He returned his attention to Amos. "Hideouts?"

Amos returned the conversation to its earlier subject. "Any trackers with those folks down yonder?"

Law hung fire before answering. He had guessed the reason for the question. "Me. I was their scout for meat and waterholes. That's how I came onto those Indians. I went up into the timber before daybreak to find a high place where I could see far out and around when daylight came."

"You're a single man, Mister Law?"

"Yep. What's your name, mister?"

"Amos Cardiff."

"Mister Cardiff, what happens now?"

"Nothing, I expect. You can't ride or walk. We'll have to talk about it."

"Mister Cardiff, we passed through a town a few days back. Took on some supplies, horseshoes, flour, whatnot. I been with those folks fourteen weeks. I know 'em pretty well. Maybe they'll find the place where your Indians was lying. Maybe they'll find some blood on the pine needles. And maybe when I don't come back after that shooting, they'll pack up and roll for that town to get some help and come back here."

Amos nodded. Probably everyone in the village had thought about that. Tenkiller's wife came over and stood gazing at David Law in long silence. It made him uncomfortable. She left the cabin as soundlessly as she had entered it. David Law watched the open doorway as though expecting her to return.

Amos said, "Good woman. They don't make 'em any better."

"She's an Indian, for chrissake."

Amos rose. "Maybe I been around 'em too long. I hadn't noticed that."

Law called when Amos was over in the doorway. "You live with them up here?"

"Yep, for many years." Amos considered the younger man's worried expression. "Mister Law, you're safer here than you was down yonder, and my guess is that you'll get better care. These folks use medicine they know will work on a man. The best I ever got from a white doctor was carbolic acid and laudanum . . . Get some sleep. They'll fetch you something to eat directly."

The day was wearing along. The initial shock of what had happened at Coffee Creek was gone. People were beginning to resume their normal activities again. There was talk, no laughter, but general discussions of things that had always been uppermost: hunting, "making meat" for winter, and gathering edible wild plants for storing.

Amos met Henry near the communal stone fire ring where the entire camp gathered occasionally to roast meat and visit. Henry had been sitting with Tenkiller, who was morose and defiant. He had told Henry someone would now have to go back down there and see what those wagon people were going to do. Henry volunteered and Tenkiller had looked pleased.

Amos listened to all this, then shrewdly said, "Well now, you don't want to go on no scout alone, and this'll give us a chance to make a sashay over where the axe man is . . . unless them other settlers rode back to his camp and told him what happened. In which case he could be fifteen miles away and still moving."

Henry considered the position of the sun while Amos spat out a cud and watched some women, including Sun Sister and Fawn, entering the Mexican's cabin.

Henry said, "We'll leave now, Amos. Go down to the axe man's place and maybe make it before dark, then bed down on the slopes heading around toward Coffee Creek and spy on them other ones at sunup."

Amos nodded. "Meet you out back at the creek in a half hour."

When they were rigged out and ready to ride, Ned Travis came ambling over to ask if they were going hunting. Amos replied that they were indeed going hunting. Ned gestured northward with a long arm. "Best place is up yonder under them icefield rims."

Amos said they might make a sashay around the lower country, come back up a few miles westward, and tomorrow hunt up near the dirty ice.

After they were riding, Amos said, "Did you hear what he said yesterday about scoutin' around down lower to see if Plume's crew was being chased? Henry, if you believe that, you'll believe anything."

Henry was looking back and did not reply. There was no sign of Sun Sister's man. Facing forward, Henry reached inside his shirt to scratch vigorously.

Their animals had been picking their way on loose reins through timber country for a long time. They required no direction until they were miles down-slope, and by the time they got down there, the forest was dark but the open grassland still had slanting daylight and heat.

They halted back in the trees, dismounted to let the horses stand easy for a while, and studied the solitary wagon out yonder. It was exactly as it had been the first time they had seen it, except that this time there was a whitish spiral of smoke rising from the stovepipe back near the tailgate, and no people were in sight.

Amos said, "Eatin' supper. We could just sort of ride in like we was pothunters." He led the way out of the trees into coppery sunlight.

Amos halloed the camp from a half mile out, and although there was no immediate response, a lean man wearing black suspenders and heavy cowhide boots emerged eventually with a long-barreled hunting rifle in the crook of one arm. Amos and Henry raised their right arms, palms forward. The axe man did the same, but did not lean his rifle aside even after they had stopped about twenty feet from the tailgate where he was standing.

Amos leaned politely aside to expectorate, then smiled as he said, " 'Evening. We're lookin' for antelope, seen the wagon, and come over to set a spell." He jutted his jaw Indian fashion at the stovepipe. "We didn't mean to interrupt your supper. This here is Henry Potter and I'm Amos Cardiff."

The axe man was average height, younger than either Amos or Henry by about twenty-five years. There was a sprinkling of gray at his temples, otherwise he had curly brown hair and brown eyes. He invited them to alight and seemed friendly, but he still did not put the rifle aside. When they were on the ground he finally spoke. "I'm Gus Muller." He gestured with his free arm. "It took us a while, but we finally located some white rocks and measured back from 'em to drive stakes. We bought this land from the railroad company." Finally, the axe man put his rifle aside. "They said there was a spring on the land but there ain't. We've walked over every yard of it and never even found where there could have been water."

A sturdy woman came from the front of the wagon, smiling as she walked back toward the tailgate. She was younger than the axe man, with reddish hair, green eyes, and freckles. He introduced her to Amos and Henry. "This here is my wife, Colleen."

The older men swept off their hats, told her their names, and when she invited them to eat, Henry said, "If it'd be all right with you folks, we'll just make camp out a few yards." They were not pressed to do othewise, but as they were parting, Gus Muller called over that after supper he'd treat them to some popskull.

By the time the horses had been unburdened and hobbled, camp made, and a meal cooked, dusk was blanketing the broad sea of grass.

Gus Muller walked over with a stoneware jug. This time he was wearing a shellbelt and holstered sidearm as well as an old hat and a coat. Henry stoked up the fire, and they talked about hunting, about the roundabout country, while passing Muller's jug around. When Muller eventually said he hadn't seen any antelope since he'd come out here about a month earlier, Amos asked him if he'd met any other settlers. Muller wagged his head. "Saw some wagons pass a while back, but they didn't stop. They was maybe a mile or so southward, goin' around the curve of the mountains. There's a creek over there. I rode over to it a couple days before I saw those folks."

"Did they come back this way?" Henry asked.

Muller shook his head. "No. No tellin' where they went. There's a lot of country hereabouts. Miles an' miles of it. If they was settlers, maybe they're still traveling."

Amos passed the jug back to Muller as he said, "Must be lonely, not seein' anyone for weeks on end."

Muller passed the jug to Henry before answering. "I been too busy for that, Mister Cardiff. I staked out where the cabin will set and rode along the foot of the hills puttin' blazes on trees I figure to use for my buildings. But what I got to do before anything else is dig a well. I been haulin' water from that creek miles west of here. Got enough to last another week, so I'll get to digging." Gus Muller passed up the jug as it came back his way. "If I don't get water there's no sense in stayin', is there?"

Amos agreed. "No sense at all. A man's got to have water before he has anything else . . . No visitors at all, eh?"

Gus Muller accepted the jug from Henry and put it aside. "No. But when I was lookin' for buildin' logs I came onto some horse tracks back in the timber a short ways, like someone had ridden downhill then turned westerly along my property line." Muller gazed at the older man. "You gents been in this area long? They got outlaws skulkin' around out here?"

Amos replied because Henry was puffing like a bellows to get his little pipe going. "I expect there's outlaws just about everywhere, Mister Muller, but as long as he went past and was hid up there in the trees, I'd say you're safe enough."

Later, after Muller had taken his jug back to the wagon with him and Henry was unrolling his blankets, Amos said,

"Well now, do you think Muller was the feller you saw that night out by Ned's corral?"

Henry shrugged. "About the same size and build, but hell, so are maybe half the fellers in the world. If it wasn't this one, Amos, then who in the hell was it?" Henry finished with the blanket-roll and sat on it to tug off his boots.

"That's the damned mystery," Amos said. "Muller don't seem to be a liar, but anyone with somethin' to hide will lie. Only I just don't feel that Muller's the man. So why was Ned prowling around down here—sure as hell he knows these folks is out here. I keep thinkin' that when he split off from Plume after that damned raid and come ridin' around here before turning north up into the mountain, he passed this camp. Why?"

Henry's pipe had gone out despite his best effort to keep it alight. He resignedly knocked it empty on a rock and pocketed it. "I don't know." He tossed down his hat, scratched his head, rolled his shellbelt and weapon to put them aside, and said, "Unless you want me to make a guess."

Amos looked up. "Guess? Guess about what?"

"That's a mighty fine lookin' redheaded woman, Amos."

CHAPTER 6
Scouting

Their animals were burdened, there was heat in the lower country, and they were in no great hurry, so they poked along; some of the time they angled uphill into timber shade for relief from the heat, some of the time rode out a ways so they could see in all directions. For these reasons they did not make the dogleg bend where the hulking mountain curved northwesterly until late in the afternoon, and they did not have the creek willows and wagon camp in sight at Coffee Creek until later, when sunlight was a slanting spectrum of faint copper and dusty rose.

There were two tall lads out with the livestock, harness horses, saddle animals, four big mules, and one or two milk cows. These settlers chose to eat around a communal fire ring. There were some women making kindling when Amos and Henry heard someone raise the call. They stopped a ways out and waited. Men congregated on the east side of the wagon camp, armed, silent, and motionless. Amos sighed, spat, and said, "The Muller man didn't know nothing. These here folks act the way folks in wagon camps used to act when they saw Indians. Be careful, partner."

Henry did not respond. He raised his right arm high, kneed his horse into a plodding walk, and approached the camp, where the men appeared to be more curious than worried. They invited Amos and Henry to dismount, tie their horses, and come into camp.

Amos tried to count the people, but gave up because

youngsters were in and out of wagons, scooting beneath them, or running out where the livestock grazed. The women, too, did not stand still to be counted.

The spokesman for the wagoneers was a big, rawboned, craggy-faced man named Hugh Morton. He invited Amos and Henry to sit near the stone ring where the women were doing their chores again as though two weatherbeaten, shaggy-headed strangers wearing belt knives, holstered pistols, and carrying saddleguns were everyday visitors. But occasionally one of them would cast a sidelong glance over to where the men were sitting.

North of the wagons stood the massive log house the original settler on Coffee Creek had constructed. It was chinked with mud, had a sod roof from which grass was growing thinly, and was ugly as original sin, but to Henry's eyes it was as impregnable as a fort.

They told the same story to the silent and solemn wagon men they had told the other settler: they were pothunters.

Nothing was said of the missing scout or the presence of attackers up the northwesterly slope until after supper and a jug was being passed around. For more than an hour the wagon men asked questions about the roundabout country, about water, about that town they'd bought supplies at, about law enforcement, hunting prospects, and the length and severity of the winters.

Amos and Henry did not lie much, but they exaggerated. Winters sometimes had snowdrifts five feet high; spring often didn't come until late June; there was no doctor if folks got the fevers or the flux; the Law rarely ventured beyond the town limits of Bent's Siding. But the summers were wonderful, and there was probably water if a man wanted to dig for it.

Darkness had settled—men had brought armloads of wood and the women had shooed their young ones off to bed, leaving the men alone at the fire—when the big man named Hugh Morton finally said renegades had been hiding up yonder and their hired scout was missing. They'd gone up there and found blood, disturbed places where men had been lying, and tracks of an unshod horse.

Henry's eyes widened. "For a damned fact? When?"

A grizzled older man with a full-flowing speckled beard answered, "Couple of days ago."

Henry still looked incredulous as he asked another question. "You tracked 'em?"

The old man shook his head without meeting Henry's gaze. "No. Mister, we're from Pennsylvania, where they got trees but not like out here. It was dark and still as death up in there."

Hugh Morton added a little more. "The feller who owns that log house—his name is Charley Knight—he left that same night for the town back yonder. He's been out here for a while, knows folks over there. He aims to raise some possemen if he can. Tell me something, Mister Potter—where's the nearest army post?"

Henry replied matter-of-factly. "That'd be Fort Pickens. It's about sixty, seventy miles southwest, down where the regular emigrant trail passes through. But I don't think there are many soldiers down there anymore. Not since the Indian wars ended about six, eight years ago."

He met Amos's glance and looked away as one of the other settlers spoke. "You fellers seem to know this country. You ever heard of bands of renegades out here?"

Henry answered truthfully. "Years ago, there were, but as far as I know there aren't none anymore."

"Well," responded the speaker dryly. "There is now, friend."

There was no more talk until the jug had gone around and a rangy, tousle-headed younger man placed more wood on the fire. Finally, as two of the men arose and walked out into the darkness, Hugh Morton said, "That scout we lost . . . What bothers me is that we didn't find him wounded or dead up there. I don't recollect ever hearing of renegades takin' someone off with them, except women. Have you, Mister Cardiff?"

Amos shook his head without speaking because he was getting a cud tongued into his cheek. Henry answered for him. "It don't seem reasonable. Are you sure he isn't lyin' up there, maybe hid by some underbrush or deadfall?"

The old man with the full beard shifted his seat when he said, "We didn't look real hard. To tell you boys the truth, it was awful quiet and dark up in there. Them scoundrels could have been lyin' in wait. Gents, renegades can't be hung no higher for murderin' twelve men than for murderin' one man."

Amos sprayed juice into the fire, causing it to hiss. He sounded hearty when he said, "It's good soil, gents. Damned few boulders, rains in summertime. I expect folks who know about plowing and growing things could do real well out here. Maybe the growin' season's a mite short, but farming folks would know how to get around that, wouldn't they?"

Hugh Morton raised his big head to regard Amos as he spoke. "What we can't figure out is why them renegades was after us when there's a single wagon eastward around the mountain, sittin' there all by itself. That'd be easy to attack. A lot easier than our outfit."

Henry shrugged and worked at stuffing his little pipe. "If you'd like, me and Amos will scout around up in the timber tomorrow, see if we can find your scout." He paused long enough to light up, using a firebrand from the stone ring, then he puffed hard, got up a good head of smoke, and removed the pipe to also say, "But I'd guess your renegades are a hundred miles from here by now and still riding. Gents, if they'd wanted to raid you, sounds to me like they could have done it anytime before sunrise. But they didn't."

Evidently this theory had circulated among the settlers, because several of them solemnly nodded their heads and none of the others offered to disagree.

Amos was a lot less worried about these people than he

was about the man named Charley Knight who had ridden for help down at Bent's Siding. When the palaver eventually broke up, Amos went with Henry to care for their animals, tote their blanket-rolls out a way, and prepare to bed down. Finally, he mentioned his concern about the man who had not been at the firing.

Henry's response was a surprise. He was angry. "That dog-eatin' son-of-a-bitch Plume! I *told* Tenkiller! Hell's fire, Amos, he knew better'n send a party down here under Plume. You know what I think? That damned old man wanted trouble with these folks. When I talked with him in his cabin he had a sly look on his face. He knew I was against lettin' Plume come down here. But he sent him anyway. Now how in hell could it have been any other way, than that Tenkiller wanted a fight?"

Amos was too surprised at his old friend's wrath to answer until he'd unrolled his blankets and shed his boots, shellbelt, and greasy old hat. Then he shook his head at Henry and used a soothing tone when he replied. "Partner, it's done. It happened. Plume's always been a hotheaded damned fool, in my mind, but it's done, so gettin' roiled up isn't going to do any good. It's what's ahead that troubles me. Sure as I'm settin' here gettin' cold, Charley Knight will stir up those folks at Bent's Siding. It's our damned bad luck that we didn't know he was riding down there the other night or we could have caught him. But that's done too. What we got to do is figure some way to stop a goddamn war."

Henry did not respond; he rolled into his blankets, grunted like an old boar, and went to sleep.

Amos also slept, but not until he had watched a tremendous meteor of dazzling brilliance plunge across the underbelly of the heavens.

Wolves scouted up the camp, perhaps attracted by the earlier scent of cooking meat. They pad-footed their way soundlessly out of the forest through stirrup-high summer grass, in the direction of the grazing livestock, causing abject fear out there, but they did not come close enough to cause a stampede. In fact no one knew they had visited until some half-grown boys went out through dew-drenched undergrowth just short of first light and found the tracks—instead of continuing out, the boys turned back and ran to rouse everyone with their yells.

Amos and Henry were already making a little breakfast fire when the camp erupted with shouts and curses. They watched for a while, then went to work making coffee and fried meat. Amos's only comment was to the effect that instead of posting guards at night like anyone with a grain of sense would have done after their other trouble, these people waited until something else happened, then went off in all directions like headless chickens.

Henry, whose mood was better this morning, watched the excitement and laughed. He did not comment until they had thanked the Pennsylvanians for their hospitality and were about a mile on around the curve of the mountain ready to head up into the timber. Then all he said was, "At least they won't bother the meadow camp. I got the feelin' last night you couldn't get 'em to scout up into this high country for a bag of gold, and they aren't goin' to move fifty yards from them wagons until Charley Knight gets back."

It was still chilly in the timber, so neither man removed his old riding coat for several hours. They were in familiar country again. Henry had told Hugh Morton that if they found the missing scout they would bring him back to the wagon camp. If not, they would keep on their way.

They were crossing a sump-spring clearing where pines and firs could not grow because soggy soil rotted their roots, when Henry brought up a subject that had been in both their minds for several days.

"All right, now we know about the axe man and those Coffee Creek folks. What I'd give a silver cartwheel to know about now is who that feller was Ned met out behind his cabin at the corral. Sure as hell he didn't come from Coffee Creek, and I'd stake my life he wasn't the axe man."

Amos was chewing. He was pleasantly warm. His stomach had no pleats in it and he wasn't thirsty, so he remained silent.

Henry twisted in the saddle. "You all right?"

"Yep. Just fine."

"Did you hear what I said?"

"Yep."

"What you got to say about it?"

"Nothing. Just square around up there and ride your horse. Everything we got to say we've already said. Some of it more'n once."

Henry squared around and rode in silence while the climbing sun soared and eventually began its decent. He knew where they could camp when the time came and aimed for that particular spot. They could have made it back to the big meadow by pushing their animals, but they did not make the effort.

The sunlight departed as it always did in timbered high country: one hour it was there, the next hour it was not, and there was no interim period before the chill arrived.

The place where they camped had a little emeraldlike meadow with a rivulet no more than two feet across. The water was so cold it hurt a man's teeth, but the horses stood beside it drinking, resting, then drinking more. There were mosquitoes, but once the supper fire was lighted they departed.

Amos was bringing water for coffee back from the creek when Henry sat back, looking up at him. "We should be ridin' in the opposite direction," he said.

Amos knelt, put ground coffee into the water, arranged rocks to put the pan on, and flagged smoke away with his hat. "Riding where? We been up there too long, Henry. We got memories everywhere you look. And if we kept on going . . . How about Sun Sister, Tenkiller's woman, some of the others? They wouldn't know that Knight feller went after men from Bent's Siding."

"They'd know, Amos. Settlers and townsmen comin' into the mountains would make enough noise to raise the dead."

"Yeah. After they was already into the mountains. That would be too late." Amos moved away from the smoke. "If we got to leave, at least they deserve to be warned."

Henry turned the meat with his belt knife. "I'll tell you something, partner—it'd be easier not to go back than it would be to go up there, give the warning, then leave."

Amos did not deny that. He rummaged for the tin cups, filled them with coffee, and handed one to Henry. As he did this he met his friend's gaze, very gently shook his head, filled his own cup, and moved the coffee pan so it would not be directly over the fire.

Henry blew on the coffee then tried it, found it not too hot, and drank the cup half empty before putting the cup aside and speaking again. "All right. We'll stay. You remember what I'm about to say. If we're lucky, we'll live to regret it. Most likely we won't live that long."

"It's not just him, it's Plume and a handful of others. The rest of them was never in a real fight. Not the kind we been through fifteen, twenty years back."

"Tenkiller has."

"Yeah, the damned old fool. If anybody knows, he ought to. But he's a full-blood. He's an old bloody-hand. You've known them before."

Amos changed the subject. "Those Coffee Creek people got some real nice horses. Did you notice that?"

Henry suddenly laughed. "What would we do with them? We already got some good horses—as many as I like cuttin' wild hay for."

Amos grinned, pulled a soiled sleeve across his mouth, and put the empty plate aside. "Trade 'em."

"For what? Amos, I don't want another woman, an' if you're thinkin' about one, you're gettin' crazier'n I figured."

The conversation ended when they heard a bear ripping through a tree trunk in the westerly middle distance. They looked at each other. They'd been living free most of their lives and had never before heard a bear hunting grubs under tree bark in the darkness.

The bear stopped clawing. They heard him sniffing loudly just before he turned and went crashing through underbrush and small trees in great haste. Man scent had frightened him.

For a while they discussed this very unusual event, then rolled out their blankets and let the fire die.

CHAPTER 7
First Blood!

Ned Travis was gone; his woman told them he'd gone hunting. Andy Mullins and Plume were sitting in the shade and glanced up as Amos and Henry rode by. Tenkiller was sitting in front of his cabin, soaking up warmth, while his woman was busy with a stone metate and a little iron mixing bowl.

Henry and Amos cared for their animals first, left their gatherings just inside the doorway of their shacks, then went over to Tenkiller.

He nodded to them and motioned toward some fir rounds used as seats.

They told him about the people at Coffee Creek. They also told him about the man named Knight riding to Bent's Siding for help. Fawn stopped mixing and looked up. Her man sat in silence, dark eyes hidden behind the half-droop of eyelids. When he spoke it had nothing to do with what they had reported. He rocked his head sideward, northward, and said, "That white man is doing well. Fawn and Sun Sister fixed him. He's weak, but eats like a horse and can move if they help him."

Henry nodded. "How about the Mexican?"

Again Tenkiller's woman looked up as her husband pushed straighter on the bench to answer, "Dead."

Henry and Amos were shocked, and probably showed it to the shrewd, steady gaze they were getting from the old Indian. Fawn arose, disappeared inside the house, and did not return.

A dogfight erupted and continued until some large boys waded in and broke it up with kicks. Tenkiller jutted his chin in the direction of the shade where Andrew Mullins and Plume were sitting. "They want to shoot the white man," he said.

Amos dug for his tobacco and methodically examined it for dirt before skiving off a piece with his belt knife.

Henry removed his hat to beat dust from it against his leg. Neither of them met the old full-blood's gaze nor said a word until he spoke again.

"There are others who want to kill the white man, then go back down to Coffee Creek."

Henry looked briefly at his partner. The same thought occurred to them both. *A full-fledged attack in the tradition of the bloody-hands.* Henry dumped the hat back atop his head and looked directly at the old man as he said, "Tenkiller, my guess is that if they left right now, this afternoon, by the time they got down there the man who made the log house will have come back with armed riders from Bent's Siding."

Amos put in his bit. "If you let 'em go, you'd better tell 'em where we'll be on the trail north. We got to get away, and damned soon."

Tenkiller's woman emerged from the cabin without looking at them and walked northward in the direction of the Mexican's cabin. She disappeared inside.

The old man watched her, then faced forward to speak again. "Fawn's been talking among the women—that's something else that never used to be. Women made trouble, they got whipped." He eased back with his heavy shoulders against bearskin. He seemed lost in thought.

Henry and Amos stood up; the movement drew Tenkiller's black eyes upward to their faces. Amos said, "Will you let Plume go back down there?"

Tenkiller's gaze did not waver. "It never used to be—two sides in a camp making the people face off against one another. Plume? Henry, the last time we talked you told me you knew Plume. All right. I know him too. If I forbid him to go, do you think he will not do it?"

Henry glanced up to where Plume and Andrew Mullins were still sitting together, palavering in the shade. He looked back and shook his head.

Tenkiller barely inclined his head in agreement, but his gaze was narrowed and sly. "The Mexican is dead. The white man is alive. Those settlers at Coffee Creek are still down there. They hurt us, we didn't hurt them."

Amos was expressionless when he replied. "It's not just those folks. The feelin' I got about them was that they wouldn't have spirit enough to come into the mountains anyway. It's armed men Charley Knight will bring back from the town. Maybe a lot of them. Tenkiller, so far we've lost one man. They haven't lost even their damned scout. We can take him down there and give him back to them."

"He will tell them we are up here," the old man growled.

Amos reddened but kept his voice quiet. "Yes. But we got a right."

Tenkiller's expression changed. He did not tolerate arguments very well and never had. "We're Indians, Amos. We got no rights."

"No! We are whites and 'breeds, damned precious few full-bloods. There are dozens of villages with folks like we got up here. We been here a long time. I don't care if the army comes, Tenkiller, we're not outlaws. We got a right to live in our village."

Plume and Andy Mullins had left their tree shade and were approaching. They had been watching from a distance, had sensed the argument, and were coming to take part in it.

Henry shifted stance, stood hip-shot, thumbs hooked in his belt as he regarded the old spokesman. Before Plume and his companion arrived, he said, "It's up to you. If we don't run, they can't chase us like wolves after a crippled doe. If we do run, they'll come in full throat. And Tenkiller, we couldn't even get to Canada. They got the singing wires. The fastest horse on earth can't outrun wireless messages. Let us take the scout back down there."

The old man's reply was brusque. "They would still come up here."

Plume and Mullins were standing slightly to one side, listening as Henry answered the old man. "Someday they would come anyway. That's one thing that's sure as death. Someday. That will be the price we got to pay for being here, but if Plume raids now, when they come this time they won't leave a damned thing standing. Tenkiller, you've seen it before. So have we. They shoot everything that moves, steal what they can carry and set fire to everything else. You want that?"

Amos nudged his friend. They walked back across the open place, leaving the two full-bloods and the white renegade gazing after them.

Mullins, a pot-bellied, slovenly man wanted for crimes outside the mountains, spat. While watching the two men walking toward their cabins Mullins told Tenkiller, "They're turning. They got no stomach for nothin' anymore but arguin' and talkin'." He faced the old Indian on the bench.

Tenkiller told them what Amos and Henry had reported about the Coffee Creek settlers sending for reinforcements from Bent's Siding; that kept both his listeners silent for a long while.

Fawn returned, ignored all three idlers, and went inside the cabin. A few minutes later she called for Tenkiller to come in and eat.

Plume and Andy Mullins ambled back across the open place, heads down and talking. Several men were waiting when they reached the shade again. The day was waning. It was still warm, but that was not going to last much longer.

Henry and Amos sat in early dusk inside Amos's house, drinking watered whiskey and scarcely speaking until Amos straightened up so that he could see across the clearing to the cabins on the far side. He swore. "Mullins just went into the Mexican's cabin." Amos stood up, hitched his shellbelt around, and shook his head. Henry followed him out into the waning light, fragmented where it filtered through the treetops.

Among the cabins, of which there were about fifteen, a few people were in sight, mostly youngsters who hadn't been called to supper yet.

The cabin door was half open when they got there, and a man's growly voice could be heard when Amos and Henry halted. "You got one chance, mister. You come with us. We'll send you out where they can see you."

The answer Mullins got was sharp. "You're crazy. They ain't going to be just sitting around, not after they heard the shooting and I come up missing."

Mullins answered that bluntly. "You better hope that's what they'll be doin', because when we turn you loose, mister, your back will be to us all the way."

Amos brushed his partner's arm and moved into the doorway, blocking the light. Mullins turned. Henry pushed past and moved to one side. The eyes of the man on the pallet got big.

Amos took three slow steps and stopped squarely in front of Mullins. "You fool," Amos said quietly, looking him directly in the eye. "How many men'll ride with you an' Plume? Four, five, maybe six or seven? There's twelve settlers down there."

"Yallerbellies."

Amos continued as though the renegade had not spoken. "By now the man who built the log house could be back from Bent's Siding with help. Maybe ten more."

"Won't make no difference if there's fifty more," Mullins said angrily. "We're goin' to get all the horses first. Set 'em afoot. Then we're going to fire the wagons to get targets by firelight."

The other three men stared. Henry was back near the

door when he said, "For chrissake, Andy. You're goin' to start a damned war."

Mullins's thin upper lip pulled back from his teeth in a menacing smile. "Nobody knows these mountains for two hunnert miles in every direction better'n we do. If they try to find us we'll cut 'em to pieces, one and two at a time."

Amos slowly turned to gaze at his partner, then he faced Mullins again. "Does Tenkiller know about this?"

Mullins hitched at his sagging britches before replying. "He knows we're goin' down there tonight to run off their livestock."

Amos turned toward the man on the pallet. Law stared back in silent fear. He hadn't moved a muscle, had not even appeared to be breathing since Amos and Henry entered the cabin.

Mullins interpreted Amos's silence as indecisiveness and reached with a thick hand to tap Amos on the chest. He was sneering, ready to speak, when Amos's right fist came up in a blur of shadowy movement. The blow caught Mullins alongside his left jaw and knocked him violently backward. He tripped and fell against the far wall, slid off it, and rolled facedown.

For three seconds there was not a sound in the cabin. Amos rubbed his right knuckles with the palm of his left hand as he went over, toed Mullins over onto his back, and leaned over him. There was a streak of blood from the corner of the unconscious man's mouth up his cheek.

David Law, Henry, and Amos were staring at the inert body when Ned appeared at the doorway. He said, "You better disarm him, Amos. Take his pistol and knife, otherwise when he comes to his senses he'll stalk you."

Ned Travis moved a couple of feet into the room, ignored David Law and Henry, shook his head annoyedly when Amos did not take Mullins's weapons, and crossed over to disarm the unconscious man himself. As he gazed at Mullins in the waning light he said, "For an old gaffer, you hit like a kickin' mule."

Amos went over by the door, still rubbing his right hand, and looked at the man on the pallet. "Can you sit a horse?"

Law sat up, nodding his head.

Henry said, "Keep 'em both here. I'll bring back an animal."

Outside, dusk was settling, which meant full darkness was not far off. Inside, Ned Travis lighted a candle, placed it on the table, and eyed Amos, who had watched everything Travis did without blinking.

Ned sat down and said, "Is it a secret, Amos? Why did you hit him?"

"Him, Plume, and some others were goin' to go down to Coffee Creek, use this feller as bait, run off the livestock, set fire to the wagons, and shoot the people."

Ned sat motionless for a long time. "Why?"

"Because the Mexican died, but mostly because they're crazy. Good gawd, folks can't do those things anymore. And those settlers sent to the Siding for armed helpers. Plume's goin' to get himself and a hell of a lot of other people killed just because he's got some notion he's got to count a big coup. Be a big strongheart."

"Does Tenkiller know?"

"He knows part of it. I doubt he knows they're figurin' on a massacre."

Ned reached slowly for his tobacco and went to work rolling a cigarette.

CHAPTER 8
"What the Hell Is Going On?"

Amos helped David Law get dressed and made certain his poulticed bandage was firmly in place; when Henry appeared like a ghost in the doorway Amos told Ned Travis to walk outside with Henry while he helped the wounded man.

There were lights showing among the cabins; fragrant wood smoke tainted the chilly night air. Ned made no attempt to walk away nor did he speak until Amos was helping Law astride the stout mule-nosed bay and growled for Ned to get over on the far side in case Law fell. Ned moved up, looked at the wounded man, and said, "Amos, if he gets three miles I'll eat crow."

Law looked downward at the lanky man. "Next time we meet I'll bring you some salt." He gathered the reins, but Henry yanked enough slack to lead the horse by, took him around behind the cabin, and pointed with an upraised arm directly across the meadow. "Don't make noise. Don't stop, not even to pee, until you're back down out of here."

Law stared at Henry. "What'll happen when they find I'm gone?"

"Not a hell of a lot if you make good time. They can't track you in the dark."

"They'll sure as hell know where I'm heading."

"Can't be helped," stated Henry. "If you don't fall off or stop, you'll most likely have enough of a head start so they can't catch you . . . Mister Law, when you get down there, tell those folks to fort up. Tell 'em that no matter what anyone says, don't come up into the timber. Fort up and wait. Now ride!"

As the captive kneed his horse out across the broadest part of the big meadow, Ned Travis said, "You'n Amos should have gone with him. When the old man and Plume find out what you done they'll skin you alive."

Amos had been thinking about that and blamed himself. "If the son of a bitch hadn't rapped me in the chest . . ." He gestured for Ned to walk ahead and herded him back to the cabin.

Mullins was gone.

Ned turned and said sardonically, "My guess is that you gents got maybe ten minutes."

His guess was wrong. Four men were approaching the Mexican's cabin, talking softly because they clearly had no idea the captive was gone. Mullins was not among them, and their leader was the burly full-blood, Plume. They were armed, coated, and ready for the nights' work.

Ned Travis stepped to a bench and sat down. He smiled in the extremely feeble light cast by the only lit candle as Henry stepped back to peer around the doorjamb and slowly pull back. "Four of 'em," he said softly, and Amos, who had rarely taken his eyes off Ned Travis, did so now as he moved to the north side of the doorway to wait. Henry was on the south side.

Ned Travis had his own gun as well as the big knife and pistol he'd taken from Mullins. He had not acted the least bit agitated since entering the cabin and did not act that way now as Plume stepped inside and saw him sitting over there.

Three 'breeds entered behind the full-blood. Seeing Ned sitting in the gloom surprised them. He slowly raised an arm in the direction of the pallet, which was rumpled and empty. The raiders looked over there. Behind them two handguns were cocked. Plume seemed paralyzed; so did his companions. Travis addressed Plume. "You got a knack for gettin' caught out by whiteskins."

The 'breeds were waiting for their leader to do something. He did: he turned very slowly until he could make out Amos and Henry behind him against the east wall, guns raised and as steady as stones. For a long moment he looked steadily from one man to the other, then he shook his head and spoke. "I told Tenkiller not to believe you, not to trust you."

Henry, who had been wondering what to do with the raiders, answered coldly. "You lied to him, Plume. You wasn't goin' back down there just to run off the horses."

Plume ignored that statement. "You two turned the captive loose. How long ago?"

Amos answered, "Lie down on your bellies with your arms out from your sides.

The raiders did not move. Amos aimed his gun barrel at Plume's chest. They still did not move. Ned Travis grinned. "You better shoot 'em, Amos. You're not going to get no cooperation unless you do."

From out front a man called guardedly. "Plume, you in there? It was Amos and Henry. Amos hit me and when I come around the prisoner was gone . . . Plume?"

Ned lowered his voice and called back. "Come in here."

Mullins stepped past the doorway, saw Ned sitting across the room, saw Plume and his companions staring in the direction of the east wall, and very slowly turned.

He looked like he would faint when he saw the men with cocked six-guns on either side of the door he'd just come through. Amos wigwagged with his gun barrel. "Disarm 'em, Andy. Do it from behind. Don't get between us and them. *Move!*"

The raiders did not resist being disarmed. They might have, at least Plume might have, except that as Mullins shuffled around behind him, Ned Travis said the same thing Henry and Amos had said. "Don't get between me and them, you damned fool."

Ned finally arose to walk forward and start picking up belt guns. He did not bother with the knives. When he stopped in front of Plume he exchanged a long stare with the warrior, then wagged his head and went toward the doorway. "Now what?" he asked Amos.

"Gag 'em and leave 'em tied up in here, then get the hell out of here."

Ned turned back smiling. "You first, Plume."

The full-blood stared at Ned. He was still having difficulty accepting the fact that Ned was siding with the older men. He had heatedly argued with Tenkiller about the loyalty of Henry and Amos, but he'd never for a moment expected Ned Travis to be in sympathy with them. He said, "You went down to Coffee Creek with us. You been on other raids with me. Now you are betraying us."

Ned pointed earthward with his barrel. "Lie down or I'll blow your head off."

Plume sneered, "No, you won't. It would bring the whole camp down here."

Ned barely allowed him to get the last word out when he swung the gun barrel sideways. Plume dropped without a sound, blood appearing in the coarse black hair above his temple.

Amos and Henry were big-eyed as Ned turned and cocked his handgun. The three 'breeds dropped belly-down and pushed out their arms.

The older men rummaged for ropes, tore cloth to make gags, and finished without saying a word. But when they were standing up again, Henry scrowled at Ned. "You know what'll happen to you and your woman for helpin' us?"

Ned did not reply. He went to the door, leaned to look out, then jerked his head. "Get saddled, meet me behind my place as quick as you can."

Amos scowled. "What about Sun Sister?"

"She'll come with us. Goddammit, do like I say." Ned faced around in the pale light. He was no longer smiling. His expression was murderous. "Don't stand there looking like idiots. Go! I'll be ready in ten minutes and you two better be ready or we're going out of here without you. For chrissake . . . *go!*"

Amos pushed past the younger man, followed by Henry. As they hurried across the starlit clearing Amos looked around. "What the hell is goin' on? Do you understand this?"

Henry didn't. "Never mind that. I never trusted him either, but right now that don't matter. Fill your saddlebags, leave everything that's heavy—and be thankful he took them raiders by surprise."

"They warn't any more surprised than I was. Since I've known him, Ned's never done nothin' without a reason. Henry, I thought he was our prisoner when he come in over there."

"Go get your horse."

"I'll ride one and lead the other one." Just before they parted, Amos asked, "Where did you get that horse we put the captive on?"

"Out of old Tenkiller's corral. He had nine of them. Now he's got eight."

Amos stared. "You stole one of the old man's horses?"

They split off, still hurrying. Henry bypassed his house to reach the corral, then swiftly rigged out his animal, left it standing, and scuttled back to the cabin to fill his saddlebags with the few articles he treasured most. He left everything else and returned to slap the bags behind his cantle, tie them into place, mount up, and walk his horse northward until he could see Amos on the ground beside a saddle horse. He swung up with a rope shank in his right hand. It went back to the squaw bridle he'd fashioned over the head of the led horse.

An owl sounded up through the trees over near the creek. Without a word both the older men rode in that direction.

Ned was up there with Sun Sister, both mounted, with bulging saddlebags tied in place. Without a word being said,

Ned led off, winding northward up through the timber, bearing well clear of the settlement and the other corrals with horses in them. He did not alter course for an hour, by which time Amos and Henry were getting worried.

Finally, Ned reined off directly westward. They were skirting around the big meadow, staying close enough to have dark forest on their right as they angled around toward the distant game trails that passed deeper into the trees.

No one spoke until they were well into the timber and following a crooked but well-traveled deer trail. Ned turned and looked past Sun Sister, who rode directly behind him, to where Henry rode in front of Amos. "Depends on how long they struggled to work free back there. But they'll be comin' long before we reach Coffee Creek."

Henry said nothing. Amos was occupied with both hands and looped reins until he got a chew into place, then, as he unlooped the reins, he said, "Why did you buy in, Ned?"

Ned straightened forward in the saddle without answering. His woman acted as though she had heard none of what had been said. She was probably still too stunned and bewildered to think very much at all.

The land eventually tipped where the high plateau country gave way to the Coffee Creek watershed. From here on they would be riding down-slope.

It was cold, so they bundled up. It was also very still; so quiet in fact they could hear every hoof-fall even though their animals were treading upon layers of pine and fir needles.

Ned eventually halted on the rim of a brushy, heavily overgrown deep canyon. The trail did not go down there but angled in and out among trees and huge boulders along the canyon's rim. In broad daylight riders up there would be sitting ducks to anyone who had something in mind besides just watching them pass by.

Amos was the last rider. He occasionally looked back and listened. Only once did he hear anything that held his attention; a large animal, probably a bear, suddenly went charging blindly through underbrush. It did not have to mean anything, and the sound was distant. It only sounded close because of the utter stillness and the thin coldness of the air.

But bears that denned for the night were not inclined to leave their beds in darkness, unless something, perhaps a scent, had reached them to cause fear. About the only thing bears feared was men.

He rode twisted from the waist for as long as he could hear the frightened bear, then faced forward with a shrug. It could have been their scent that reached the bear.

If it wasn't, it was the aroused and furious riders from the big meadow, who would be a fair distance to the rear, so Amos would not say anything until he had something definite to report.

Ned switched trails and went down a steep slope at the south end of the thorny canyon, where the cold was more biting, and halted in a bosk of black oaks to wait until everyone was close. "Couple more miles," he said. "If the scout made it back, he couldn't have done it more'n a short while ago. I'm countin' on him havin' done it, and those folks bein' wide awake with lamps burning." He eyed Amos and Henry. "What do you think?"

Henry answered. "Me'n Amos will ride in first. You two stay out of sight. Those folks know us. We been down there before."

Ned gestured. "Take the lead."

From this point on, the land was not as rough nor precipitous as it had been farther back, but there was a variety of undergrowth, including wild grape and thornpin, things that wounded horses and tore cloth. It had to be painstakingly threaded through, and that took time.

Amos was chewing, his old riders' coat buttoned to the gullet. He said, "Henry, did you really steal one of the old man's horses?"

Instead of an answer, Amos got a long, scowling look.

Travis spoke from farther back. "If you did, Henry, then we got someone behind us a lot worse'n Plume. The stories I've heard about the old man when he's on a war trail would make your hair stand up."

Sun Sister, who had not made a sound since they'd left the big meadow and the village, spoke now. "Someday maybe we can go back."

Ned snorted but did not comment.

Henry rode hunched inside his old coat, hat pulled low, slate eyes squinted. This was not the route he and Amos had used after their earlier departure from the Coffee Creek settler camp; but it would take them there. What he was waiting for was any kind of sound made by people or their animals. What he eventually heard was a dog barking in the distance. It was a faint but clear sound, and Henry aimed his horse directly toward it.

The sky was faintly brightening beyond the mountains in the distant east, but where they were riding there was not even a hint of sunrise. It usually got coldest just before dawn, and by the time the barking dog sounded much closer, it was very cold. Late summer or not, predawn in high country was cold.

They smelled wood smoke. The dog was no longer barking. Henry rode another quarter mile, then signaled to Sun Sister and her man to stay where they were. Henry and Amos covered the final distance to the settler camp and rode directly toward the eerie-looking wagons in the fish-belly grayness of a new day.

CHAPTER 9
Waiting

Smoke was rising; several men and boys were visible in the distance, bringing in the livestock. Elsewhere women, bundled against the chill, were busy preparing the day's first meal and boys were out scavenging for dry wood. There was a man standing on a tailgate with a rifle. When he saw riders approaching, he whistled, and almost immediately the children disappeared, the women moved away from the communal fire ring, and the men moved warily among barrels, wagons, and trunks, only their guns showing.

Amos shook his head. "Law must've made it, Henry. They're as skittish as a bunch of schoolgirls."

Henry's reply indicated another concern. "Where in hell is Knight with his possemen from town? There's no more down there than there ever was."

Henry had raised his right arm, palm forward, as he'd aimed his mount in the direction of an opening among the wagons where several heavily armed men were waiting. He recognized two of them, the wagon boss named Hugh Morton and that wizened old scarecrow with the flowing beard.

When Amos and Henry were recognized, Morton said something and several men rolled barrels clear so they could ride inside the forted-up place. As they rode in, Morton said, "Are they behind you?"

Henry dismounted before replying. "Two friends are. We left 'em out yonder. Amos can go back and fetch them in."

Morton did not look pleased. "Who are they?"

"A feller named Travis an' his wife."

"That's all?"

"Yes."

Morton turned. "Fetch 'em, Mister Cardiff," and as Amos was reining around, the wagon boss motioned first for a gangling lad to take Henry's horse, then pointed toward a huge old blue-ware coffeepot on some rocks and trooped over there to begin filling cups. As he was doing this, solemn as a judge, taciturn and worried but resolute, the old man with the full beard came up beside Henry and said, "Dave Law come in maybe fifteen minutes back, sick as a dog. They got him in a wagon bein' tended. He told us who you fellers was and what you done up yonder."

Morton handed Henry a tin cup with steam rising from it.

Amos sipped scalding coffee without replying. The coffee was bitter as sin and stout enough to float horseshoes, but it was hot. He felt its warmth all the way to his feet.

"You boys said you was pot hunters, Mister Potter."

Henry sat on the ground. "We are."

"You never mentioned a mountain town of renegades."

"They're not renegades, Mister Morton. They are 'breeds, whites, and a handful of full-bloods."

"And," said a gaunt man leaning on a long-barreled rifle with a bird's-eye maple stock, "they're on their way to attack us."

Henry lowered the cup to the ground. "Some of 'em are, led by a full-blood named Plume. Did Law tell you about Plume?"

Several men nodded, but only Hugh Morton spoke. "He told us. He told us quite a bit. He's beholden to you gents, and now that you come here, so are we. Unless you don't aim to lend a hand when the fight starts."

Henry picked up the cup again. "Where are them posse-men Mister Knight went after?"

Morton did not know. "We haven't seen hide nor hair of Charley since he left out of here a few nights back. How long would you expect it'd take him to get over to that town, round up some riders, and come back?"

"Two days. At the most, three days. Mister Morton, is Charley Knight a drinkin' man? Because if he is, he might get a little delayed in Bent's Siding."

Morton did not answer the question, because Amos was returning with Ned Travis and Sun Sister. Everyone, even the women who had been discreetly invisible until now, came out to stare. The man with the Kentucky rifle said softly, "That there's a squaw."

Henry unwound up to his full height, waited until his companions of the night-long ride were inside and dismounting, then introduced them. Sun Sister stood very close to her man, large liquid eyes moving slowly among the settlers. Sun Sister seemed to be on the verge of fleeing until a woman no older than she was came over with a smile.

The young woman offered a hand. Sun Sister took it and was led over near one of the wagons to join the other women and the children.

At the fire ring the men were seated, listening to Ned, who had heard horsemen back up the hill in deep timber. His estimate was that they were by now probably in sight of the camp, but concealed.

Dawn had arrived; there was daylight but as yet very little warmth. Some of the men left the fire ring to pace along the barricade on the east side. The remaining settlers lingered at the fire, listening to what Ned had to say. Amos and Henry were impressed with his fluency and his easy manner. He showed less tautness and anxiety than anyone at the fire ring.

Eventually the men moved away to allow the womenfolk to make a meal. Henry went with the old man to get some drinking water, while Amos and Ned Travis strolled in the opposite direction. Sun Sister never let Ned out of her sight as she peeled potatoes beside the friendly younger woman.

The old man's name was Ben Fulbright. He sealed a friendship with Henry by offering him a pouch of rough-cut, genuine pipe tobacco. As they lit up near a water barrel lashed to the side of a big old wagon, the old man pointed with his pipe stem in the direction of the gaunt man with the handmade long-barreled rifle. "That's Luther Davis. Sort of related some way to old Jeff Davis. He was a Secesh soldier from Virginia. See that lady flaggin' her apron at the smoke? That's his wife. They own one of them long-legged boys that brought in the horses." The old man paused to tamp his pipe with a callused thumb.

Henry said, "How about you, Mister Fulbright?"

"Call me Ben. Me? I come along because I got no one back east; all dead or scattered god-knows-where by the war." Fulbright's keen blue eyes jumped to Henry's face. "You got family, Mister Potter?"

"Nope. And my name is Henry. This here is the first real tobacco I've smoked in a long while."

"Got a nice bite, don't it? I brought along a sack. Well, Henry, they're fixin' to feed us. You want another drink of water?"

"No, thanks. Ben, there's another wagon around the mountain eastward a few miles. The feller's name is—"

"They packed up and left. We waved to 'em yestiddy as they headed west. No one went out to talk to 'em. There was a redheaded woman on the seat. I've been in places where Indians would trade a lot of horses for a scalp that color so's they could make little switches of it an' sew 'em down their pants legs."

Henry trickled fragrant smoke. "So have I, but that was a while back, Ben. No war parties left now."

"Aren't there? Then what in hell are them bastards doin' sneakin' around up yonder among the trees?"

Henry had no opportunity to reply; Amos was waving his arm and calling him to eat.

Amos had been counting noses. Including half-grown lads big enough to use weapons, there were about sixteen men. He was unable to count the women accurately because, as they'd been doing before when he'd tried for a head count, some came and went among the wagons, some moved among the men to hand out tin plates of hot food, and some remained among the barricades with the sentries Morton had posted to keep watch.

He did not count the children under gun-bearing size, but thought there had to be about eight or ten of them.

When Henry came up and sat on the ground, old Ben Fulbright went around to sit opposite him between Hugh Morton and Luther Davis.

There was smoke, as there always was at a cooking fire, but without wind to stir it, for the most part it was not troublesome. Amos ate with a hearty appetite; he had been hungry the night before when they'd left the big meadow. This was compounded by the kind of meal the settler women put together: it was very good. Neither Amos nor Henry had enjoyed a genuine woman-cooked hot meal in a coon's age.

There was little talk during the meal, at least among the men, but the women kept up a lively conversation among themselves. Sun Sister understood everything they said, but remained silent. Mostly, she hovered near her man, who seemed unaware of her as he ate and drank. Later, when the meal was finished and the settlers had lit their pipes and began asking questions, he told them about the country for miles in all directions.

Amos and Henry exchanged a look. Ned acted different than he'd been up at the big meadow. Up there, he went off by himself much of the time, hunting, he had said, but as often as not he had returned without game. Here, among the settlers, he was perfectly comfortable and at ease, which neither Henry nor Amos were.

When they could do it, they left the palaver at the stone ring, ostensibly to look after the horses and put their outfits where they would not be in the way, but in reality to talk where they would not be overheard.

They did not discuss Ned, not initially; they speculated

about Plume and who else might be up there in the timber, waiting for darkness. Amos was sure old Tenkiller was up there, if for no other reason than that he had certainly discovered hours ago that it was one of his horses the wounded man had escaped on.

"And Mullins," Henry said, naming others he thought would be waiting in the forest. "They're goin' to try special hard to get you'n me, Amos."

Amos glanced beyond the wagon camp toward the dark, forbidding uplands, where nothing was visible but large trees. "Yeah. What we should have done was pack in the night, saddle up, and ride out a long time ago."

Henry scowled faintly. "I told you that weeks back, but you was too pig-headed."

Amos faced around, brows rising. "Are you sayin' I'm responsible for this fix we're in now?"

"No . . . I'd like to say it, only you'd get mad. You expect these people have some whiskey?"

Amos leaned against a large wheel near the tailgate of a wagon and crossed both arms across his chest. "You didn't fetch the bottle you kept hid in your flour bag?"

"We had to travel light, you know that."

"Whiskey in a little bottle don't weigh much."

Ned Travis strolled up, smoking a brown-paper cigarette that he removed to knock ash from as he said, "They was sweatin' for fear Plume'd raid them this morning. I told them to get plenty of rest because he'll come after dark and everyone'll want to be wide awake."

Amos eyed Ned skeptically. "Did you tell 'em to put water buckets all around? Plume, Tenkiller, and the other full-bloods won't come howlin' out of the timber, wavin' guns and wearing feathers. They'll creep down here and throw pitch bundles atop them wagons . . . Then the shootin' will start. After it's full dark."

Ned gazed at Amos with a hint of amusement showing. "We're the same," he said. "When it come right down to it, no matter about the rest of it, we side with the whites. Even old fellers like you two who ain't been around 'em in years."

Amos's expression of disapproval deepened. "White, your butt," he retorted. "Me'n Henry want to keep this from growin' into the kind of a fight that'll bring in the army, along with a mob of townsmen. We want—"

"How the hell do you expect to do that?" Ned said, stung by the older man's clear dislike.

"We'll just have to think on it," Amos replied, and strode in the direction of the water barrel because he was thirsty.

Ned watched him depart, his expression menacing. Henry brought the younger man's attention back. "Did they tell you them other folks, the ones around the slope a few miles—the settler feller with the redheaded woman—struck camp and rolled west a couple days ago?"

Ned stared at Henry, dropped his smoke and ground it savagely underfoot, looked up, and said, "Why? I thought they liked it over there."

"My guess is because they couldn't find water on their claim. You can't do much even with good ground if you don't have no water."

As Ned turned away and strolled back in the direction of the stone ring, where Hugh Morton and several men were conversing, Henry inclined his head almost imperceptibly. How would Ned know those people had liked it over there unless he had talked to them? It did not make Henry feel any better to know that he probably had been right, that Ned had visited those folks because he had been intrigued by the redheaded woman.

Sun Sister was the daughter of Henry's late wife's sister. She had been a delightful and lovely child. She was still a handsome and delightful woman. Travis wouldn't be the first white man to live with an Indian girl until he decided to ride on and did so for no reason at all except that he could do it.

Amos returned with a cud in his cheek. "The creek's a

mite far for these folks to go with buckets to refill their barrels as long as Plume's out there."

Henry brought his attention slowly back to his old friend. "That's nothin' to worry about unless they're low on water," he said.

"They are," Amos replied, watching the people at the stone ring, the heart of their camp. "Sure aren't all from one part of the country, like I thought they was, Henry."

The reply Amos got was on a different subject. "Ain't going to do any good standing' around here. If you know somethin' bad can happen, then you figure on it up ahead, don't you?"

Amos nodded, still watching the people.

"Maybe we can't do much, Amos, but tryin' is better'n waiting."

"Try what? Henry, they're watchin' every blessed thing that happens down here. They're hid up there like ticks, an' by nightfall they'll know every settler and every damned horse by sight."

Henry changed the subject again, "Let's go see if that old gent with the whiskers knows where there's a bottle of whiskey . . . Amos?"

"What?"

"What do you suppose happened to Charley Knight?"

"Hell, I got no idea."

CHAPTER 10
The Wagon Camp

Old Ben Fulbright led off with twinkling eyes. He did not halt until he was at the tailgate of a wagon, where he held up a hand to Amos and Henry, climbed over the tailgate, and reappeared within moments with an earthen jug wrapped in sacking. As he climbed back out and held up the jug to Henry he said, "Too bad the color don't show. It's like gold."

Henry swallowed twice and handed the jug to Amos, who slung it over his shoulder and turned his head as Henry eyed the old man. "By god, Mister Fulbright, that's—"

"Ben. I told you my name is Ben."

"Ben, that's the smoothest whiskey I ever tasted. You make it?"

The old man flashed worn-down teeth in a broad smile. "Made fourteen gallons of it. Only maybe four, five gallons left. We use it for snakebite, fevers, and colds."

Amos returned the jug to its owner, who put it on the tailgate without taking a drink. "That was my trade. I was a distiller. Learnt it from my paw, who had it from his paw." He eyed his new friends. "Didn't you boys have any whiskey up in that 'breed town?"

"Some," replied Henry. "Popskull. Trade whiskey. Nothing like this, Ben. And it was hard to come by. Mostly, folks stayed up there, didn't go down to that town yonder more than maybe once a year."

The old man put his head slightly to one side. "I know better'n to ask this question, but it's bein' speculated on

71

around the camp. How come you fellers to be livin' with redskins?"

Amos answered. "We had Indian wives. We been hunters most of our lives. We couldn't stay in towns, and up there the livin' was good, most of the time. And Ben, there aren't no more'n a handful of full-bloods up there. Mostly the folks are either 'breeds or whites."

"That pretty girl with Mister Travis—ain't she Indian?"

"Half, but she was born up in the big meadow and has never been out of the mountains. You folks are the first emigrants she's ever seen up close. Her name is Sun Sister."

Old Fulbright passed the jug around again. While his companions were drinking, he filled his pipe, lit it, waving away the cloud of bluish smoke. As the jug came back he said, "Folks are wonderin' if maybe them renegade friends of yours didn't catch Charley Knight on his way to that town. He should have got back by now."

Amos shook his head. "I don't think so. We didn't know he'd gone for help until we talked to Hugh Morton. By then it would have been too late to overtake him. As far as I know, no one tried to."

A buxom, graying woman with eyes as blue as cornflowers came along, nodded to Amos and Henry, wagged a finger at Ben Fulbright, and walked on. Amos's eyes followed her until she was out of sight down the side of the wagon. Ben noticed and said, "That's the widow Henderson. She's from Philadelphia. Her husband took down with the bloody flux couple months back and died. This here is her wagon. I ride with her to mind the livestock and whatnot."

Henry was eyeing the jug, but when it was offered to him again he waved it away. He managed to make a visible but silent hint by taking out his little pipe and holding it until Ben Fulbright passed over his pouch. Then, as Henry was stuffing in shag he said, "Ben, your water barrel over yonder is getting empty." He lit up and puffed hard for a moment before continuing. "That creek out there to the west is called

Coffee Creek. It might be a good idea to fill the barrels and the buckets before sundown."

Old Fulbright's keen gaze was fixed on Henry. "Fire arrows?"

"Somethin' like it. They got all afternoon to set up there cutting pitch splinters and wrapping them. They'll set fire to anything that'll burn if they're thrown in here or atop the wagon canvases."

Fulbright sucked on his pipe, then removed it. "Hugh's passed orders for no one to go outside the camp."

Henry looked at his partner, then back to Fulbright. "Has he ever been in a firefight?"

Fulbright did not think so. "They ain't had Indian trouble in Pennsylvania since his daddy's day, and out here we've only come onto raggedy-assed Indians around the towns an' settlements, mostly beggars or drunks, no fightin' Indians."

Amos sighed. "Those aren't Indians, Ben. They're mostly 'breeds and whites."

Fulbright conceded. "All right. Renegades then. What I know about renegades, gents, is that they make bronco Indians look like preachers."

"Water," Henry said. "I think me'n Amos better go talk to Mister Morton."

As Henry and Amos were walking away, Ben Fulbright tamped his pipe, gazed after them, and wagged his head. He was turning to climb back over the tailgate when the buxom woman with the silver hair and blue eyes looked out at him. "They look capable," she said.

Ben glanced over his shoulder before replying. "I'd say they are. They lived with Indians, was married to squaws, Miz Henderson. They're what folks call squaw men."

"What do you think of them?" she asked, also looking over to where Henry and Amos were talking to the wagon boss and Luther Davis.

"I'd say they're sound, ma'am. Sort of gamey lookin' but

resourceful. I'd guess they've been through just about every-thin' at least once. Some things several times."

Amelia Henderson extended a brawny arm, grasped Ben's hand, and helped him over the tailgate. Like everyone else she had been very afraid, but also like the others she could not sustain fear indefinitely, and the day had worn along since the scout had returned with his amazing and frighten-ing tale.

Now, all the settlers could do was wait and hope Charley Knight would return with armed reinforcements.

This was exactly the point Henry was trying to make with Hugh Morton. "Plume can set up there, because you're not goin' anywhere an' he knows it. He can wait and make fire bundles, maybe nap a little and wait for nightfall. Mister Morton, the reason me'n Amos are still above ground is because we never did that. If trouble was on the way, we got ready to meet it. Sometimes we'd do more'n that—hit before we got hit. Amos just told you they'll use fire bundles and you got to place buckets all around here. You got to fill your barrels."

The craggy-faced wagon boss stood in dour silence, but the gaunt, taciturn man with the long rifle said, "It's a fair hike from here to that creek. If they got rifles up there, an' they snuck down close as the last stand of trees, they could pick us off like we was rats in a granary. That's open country all the way to the creek. A man could hide among them creek willows so's they couldn't see him to aim at, but how would he get back, luggin' a bucket of water in each hand?"

Henry did not reply. What the gaunt man had said was true. Henry had not said it wouldn't be dangerous, he'd said that if the water barrels and every blessed bucket in the settler camp was not full of water when nightfall arrived, Plume's raiders would set fires so they would have light to aim by.

Luther Davis started to say more, but Morton spoke first. "I'll handle it, Luther," he said, and eyed the men from the big meadow. "Last night we could have filled the barrels by darkness, but last night we didn't know we'd have to."

Amos could not resist being sarcastic. "I'd say you're right, Mister Morton. I'd also say every wagon boss I've known never let his barrels get near to empty. I'd also make a guess that if you're thinkin' of maybe sending out a bucket brigade after sundown, if they reach the creek sure as hell they'll never reach the damned wagons on their way back. Come along, Henry."

Morton and Luther Davis stood in long silence, watching Henry and Amos walk away. Luther leaned on his rifle as he said, "I've got a notion to trust them. They've done us favors for a fact. But it's hard to look at those big belt knives along with those hide shirts and not be a little suspicious. All my life I've heard stories about renegade whites."

Hugh Morton pulled himself up into an erect stance. He was a big, powerfully put together man, thin lipped, bold eyed, and humorless. He listened to Luther in stony silence before saying, "What about the water, Luther? They're most likely right about fire bundles. They probably know about sneakin' around in the dark and hurling them onto cabin roofs and atop wagon canvas. But right now—what about the water?"

Luther mumbled that he would go among the wagons to see how much water they had, and after he had departed Hugh Morton went to the wagon tongue of a rig on the west side, sat down, and when a slight, weathered older woman came over to offer him the heel from a freshly baked loaf of bread, he accepted it with a grunt. Then he looked up at her with a visible trace of fondness showing. "Missus Morton," he said, around a mouthful of warm, fragrant bread, "we got natural beauty on all sides of us, and killin' sons of bitches mixed in with it."

She smiled at him. "Mister Morton, as far back as I can remember it's always been like that, and you've always got us through."

He chewed as she walked away, swallowed, then stood up to peer westerly, over to where Coffee Creek's inviting shallows showed through dense thickets of blackcaps and lacy creek willows. He then twisted in another direction to gauge the distance between the watercourse and the nearest ranks of forest mammoths where the sun did not penetrate. As he swallowed the last of the warm bread and reset his hat to shield his eyes from the moving sun, he spoke aloud to himself. "If a man could know how destiny works, he'd most likely never cross to the west side of the Missouri River."

Luther Davis found him standing there when he came to report that there was enough water for the livestock and the people, but that there would not be if they did as those two squaw men said: fill every blessed bucket in camp and put them where they'd be handy for putting out fires after nightfall.

Morton nodded without speaking and led the way over to the fire ring, where Sun Sister and her new friend with the roan-colored hair and green eyes were putting pans of potatoes to boil. He ignored Sun Sister to ask the other woman if the Indian lady understood English.

Sun Sister answered him. "That's the only language I know."

Morton and Davis studied her in silence for a moment before the big man asked a question: "Our scout said two women looked after him. Was you one of them?"

"Yes. Fawn Tenkiller was the other one."

Morton's eyes narrowed slightly. "Tenkiller?"

"Tenkiller is the camp spokesman of the village. He's old and scarred. Fawn is his woman."

"He a full-blood?"

"Yes. There aren't many. Tenkiller, Plume, a man named Fair Child, one called Stone."

Morton inclined his head slightly. "We got folks named Stone and Fairchild. Not here but back east. Mister Travis is your husband?"

"My man, yes."

"Well, you know those folks up yonder. Tell me what you think will get us out of this mess."

Sun Sister looked from one man to the other, then raised an arm, pointing in the direction of Henry and Amos, who were sitting on the ground in the shade of a wagon with Ben Fulbright and several other men.

Sun Sister turned away; Morton and Davis continued to gaze in the direction of the seated men. Davis sighed as though he might speak, but a man leaning on his rifle on the tailgate straightened up with an outflung arm and whistled.

There was a solitary horseman loping in from the southwest. He was riding straight up in the saddle, his animal rocking along through golden sunlight. A number of men went to the east side to watch. Henry and Amos went with them. Ned Travis came up about the time the distant horseman was straightening out for the final ride toward the wagons after coming around the out-thrusting mountain slope that cut off all viewing westerly from the wagons.

One of the watchers said, "Hell! Where's them reinforcements he was supposed to bring?"

Another settler, hand raised to shield keen eyes, made a flat statement. "That's not Charley Knight."

"Well then, who'n hell is it?"

"A stranger. That's a real fine-lookin' chestnut horse he's riding. Got a flaxen mane an' tail an' four white socks. Whoever he is, that horse cost him a lot of money."

Henry brushed Amos's arm and walked away. Their departure was not noticed by the people, whose complete interest was in the oncoming rider. They got completely across the dusty enclosure without being hailed or even noticed because now the distant rider had raised his right arm, palm forward, and was close enough for the onlookers to make out most of the details of his outfit.

One watcher stiffened and sucked in a gasp of breath as he stood squinting with the others. He abruptly eased to the rear of the crowd, went over to the barrels where Hugh was standing, rifle slanting across the bend of one arm, and said, "His name is Fred Butler. Lend a hand with these barrels."

Morton leaned aside his rifle to help roll aside the barricade. "You know him? He isn't from that big meadow is he?"

"No. He's from Bent's Siding."

Into the total stillness the report of a single gunshot sounded. It was as distinct as a muzzle blast could be. The watchers, including Ned and the wagon boss, were paralyzed with astonishment as the beautiful horse, which had been loping on a loose rein, simply continued its stride for another ten feet or so, then went slowly down to the ground.

Another gunshot sounded from northward among the trees and the man, who had landed on both feet, twisted under the agonizing impact and dropped like a stone.

Ned shifted his gaze to the puff of dirty gray gunsmoke rising down near the foremost stand of trees where they met the open country. "Shoot," he yelled in anger, raising his gun and aiming at the forest where the soiled puff of black-powder smoke was hanging. "Shoot!"

The settlers responded with a ragged flurry, mostly from rifles, since the distance was too great for handguns.

CHAPTER 11
A Deadly Contest

Amos and Henry crouched in the willows looking back. They had not seen the horse and rider go down, but they had heard the pair of gunshots that had downed them. Now, panting in their concealed place, they heard the fusillade from the wagons and tried to guess what the gunfire was about. But not for long.

Henry growled, arose into a crouch, and went swiftly up along the dogleg watercourse, remaining concealed by undergrowth as he hastened northward.

Where Coffee Creek emerged from the mountains, where it derived its water miles upland beneath some dirty icefields and granite crags, creek willows waged a futile battle against large trees and strangling stands of verdant undergrowth. They got up there covered with sweat and ready to drop to the ground from exhaustion. Amos looked over his shoulder, saw nothing behind him and heard nothing, looked ahead, and said, "That sounded like a damned war."

Henry was sluicing cold creek water over his face as he replied, "Damned short one. You rested?"

"No! You think I'm twenty years old?"

Henry turned a dripping, beard-stubbled face with little gray eyes sardonically twinkling. "A blind man couldn't make that mistake. Soak in the water, then we got to keep moving."

They remained with the creek only until they came to a trampled place where men and animals had tanked up, then turned off deeper into the timber. Now, in their element, they made good time without seeming to; they appeared as ghosts or shadows moving in fits and starts from big trees to scabby plinths of crumbly prehistoric stone, to brush patches and back among the trees.

They went up-country a half mile, quartered for sign, found it, and drifted down-country again so as to come upon their prey from behind. They were experienced at this sort of thing, and if it had ever occurred to them that the trade they had learned from redskins lacked the elements of courageous chivalry other people respected, they must have spat in contempt decades ago. Chivalry didn't matter, survival did.

They halted in forest gloom when Amos reached with a rough hand and lightly punched his companion. Amos was still crouching, but his head was up and slowly turning, testing and turning. He punched Henry again and went off almost directly northward in jerky, rapid movements until he came to a place where ugly, ancient stones had been left, perhaps by prehistoric explosions of some kind, in a large, uneven circle. Amos worked through thickets in the occasional bare places and halted to raise an arm. Henry squeezed in beside him.

Within the irregular circle horses were picking at little hidden pockets of grass. Opposite the horses, sitting on a scaly boulder about waist-high, was a long-legged, bony-shouldered youth with golden skin, black hair, dark eyes, and a battered old Winchester saddlegun.

They knew him. His name was Forest Fair Child. His mother was related to Plume and his father was called Allan Horse.

With almost imperceptible stealth they sucked back, got down, and crawled away. Where they stopped, Henry jutted his chin one way, then the other. They split up, Amos starting soundlessly around one side of the stone jumble, Henry around the other.

The light was poor, shadows filled the area, and there was

a faint, fading scent of ancient dust, probably caused by the moving horses. Most noticeably absent in this place was the sound of forest birds.

It was warm without being hot. Once there was a rattle of sound, as though the young sentry had slid down from his vantage point. Amos, who was coming around from the left, pushed into a thicket, waited a long while, then raised his head. There was no movement and the silence had returned. He continued his advance until he thought the youth could not be far ahead and raised his head very slowly.

The boulder where the sentry had been sitting was bare. He pulled back down very slowly, hunkered on his haunches to listen, then crawled around a spiny thicket where an opening showed. He pushed as close as he could get and looked past scabrous rocks on both sides to peer in at the horses. They were no longer picking grass. They were nervously alert, heads high, little ears nervously moving. But there was no sign of the tall youth.

The horses had man-scent, probably from several directions, because they were shifting stance, occasionally turning their heads.

Amos raised a sleeve to wipe off sweat, and at the same moment he heard something that made a softly abrasive sound. He lowered his arm and started to rear back to look up when the equivalent of a catamount landed squarely atop him, arms flailing, a big knife flashing briefly as Amos instinctively lashed out with both feet to move sideways. His clawing, straining attacker moved with him. Amos flung up both arms, encountered flesh and bone and gamy cloth. He twisted fiercely, caught hold of an arm above the eldow, and heaved with all his strength to peel the attacker off, but only partially succeeded.

As he was thrashing in the thicket for solid footing, a flash of silvery dullness appeared. He brought one forearm upward and forward, felt flesh yield under his blow, and hurled himself backward as the blade flashed in front of his upper body.

The underbrush broke his fall. It also engulfed him. He struggled to roll and couldn't, the thicket was too dense. The youth sprang at him, knife moving upward from the waist in a wild, disemboweling sweep.

Amos had time only to raise a leg with the knee bent. The youth was struck high in the body, and his knife hand went past Amos's head with the blade sinking into layers of spongy needles. Amos forced his solid weight atop the youth, pressing his flailing arms and legs deep into the underbrush.

Amos rode him down into the spiny growth like a horse, punched him repeatedly at the back of the neck, and when he went limp, reached far over, caught his attacker's wrist, and curled his fingers until they were buried in sinewy flesh. The knife fell clear.

To complete the job, he reversed the knife, struck the youth solidly behind the ear, then rocked back to suck air for a moment before getting unsteadily to his feet.

The horses had been attracted to the north side of their enclosure by the nearly soundless struggle. But they did not get any closer to the rocks than prudence allowed.

Henry appeared, carrying an old battered Winchester. He pushed through brush to peer at the unconscious youth and at his partner, then straightened back to shove the gun lever forward and expose an empty chamber.

Amos had his answer as to why the sentry had not shot him instead of trying to kill him with his knife. There were no bullets in his old gun.

Henry flung the useless weapon away, dragged the youth from the thicket, flopped him onto his back, and shook his head. When Forest Fair Child had been small, Henry had plaited a rawhide rope for him.

Amos cleared the thicket with bleeding scratches and torn clothing. He looked a long time at the youth, whose head was swelling on one side, then leaned over and furiously sank the attacker's big knife as hard as he could into the ground beside the inert body.

Henry ignored the youth. "How did he catch you?"

"He was atop one of those high rocks and dropped on me. Don't ask how he knew I was there. I tried to be quiet, but maybe I wasn't."

Henry jerked his head. They went on around the uneven rock clearing to a place where someone had piled thorny brush and, without a word passing between them, began energetically to pull the brush aside until an open space about six or seven feet wide showed. They paused to catch their breath. The horses inside were watching them. A couple of them took tentative steps toward the opening.

Amos and Henry walked northeastward, reached a place of close-spaced forest giants, and listened as the horses left their confining place. Amos fished around for his twist, gnawed off a piece, spat, and shook his head. "I'd have killed him if you hadn't come along."

Henry replied while listening to the departing horses. "Glad you didn't. When he was little I made toys and a little catch-rope for him."

Amos was still smoldering. "That don't mean a damn."

Henry changed the subject. "We can go back or we can stay up here, but one thing is a damned cinch—Plume got caught from behind again, and this time he got set afoot. Tenkiller will be mad as a son of a bitch."

Amos was breathing easier, but his wrath could not subside for a while yet. Henry was about to speak again when Amos swiftly raised a hand for silence.

There were five of them passing in and out of the firs, carrying rifles and saddleguns and walking in the direction of the empty scab-rock corral. Amos and Henry sank flat, scarcely breathing as the raiders went past below them a couple of hundred feet. The moment the last man was out of sight, Amos and Henry sprang to their feet and moved swiftly.

It was impossible not to leave tracks in the needles that pursuers would eventually find, but they had to keep going, because pursued men lost their advantage the moment they stopped moving.

With Henry leading now, his greatest cause of anxiety was not the men who knew by now that someone had loosed their horses and was somewhere behind them. He worried about stumbling into other raiders up ahead somewhere.

Amos brushed his arm and said, "Go north."

Henry shook his head. "They could hunt us all the way back to the big meadow and there wouldn't be no help up there." He continued southward.

Amos said no more. Occasionally he would halt to listen for pursuers, then hasten after his friend. They began to find places where men had been: trampled needles, scuffed earth, broken tree limbs.

Henry halted in a low place, where he got down on his stomach and watched their back-trail. Amos did the same. They did not see anything, but they heard enough to start them onward again; this time they were saved from an inadvertent encounter by a man running lightly downhill from them, weaving among the trees without making a sound. He looked neither left nor right. He was obviously hurrying to the place where the main handful of raiders were, to tell them that someone had let their riding animals run away.

He had probably also seen the unconscious sentry, so he would have something else to tell Plume and Tenkiller: there were enemies up in the timber somewhere, possibly behind them.

Henry did not have sufficient time to ambush the messenger, so he watched the man hasten southward, and after he had disappeared, Henry shook his head at Amos. If they weren't damned careful they were going to be cut off in all directions except the one Henry did not want to use—northward, uphill back toward the village.

Amos held up his hand, stood briefly with his head to one side, then dropped his hand and jerked his head for Henry to follow as he began moving as rapidly and carefully as he could. The raiders whom the messenger had been heading for were obviously down-country, probably close to the last ranks of trees where the two earlier gunshots had sounded. The five men who had gone up to the stone corral were on their right side, northward.

Amos's guess, more like a hope, was that if they could go westward between the two groups swiftly and promptly, they just might escape. That was his strategy, and he never once looked back to make sure Henry was behind him as he almost ran in his anxiety.

An echoing high call sounded so close that both Henry and Amos dropped flat, squirmed around facing the way they had come, and drew their handguns.

Amos would have sworn someone had seen them fleeing. Henry leaned to whisper to him. "That was Andy Mullins."

Maybe it had been, but whoever was up there evidently had been calling about something besides a sighting; perhaps about the deep imprints the fugitives had left as they had hurried downhill.

He did not appear. Amos and Henry waited for him but he did not arrive, although his high call echoed again as they were getting to their feet to continue southward.

They did not come into speckled sunshine near Coffee Creek, but they could hear the creek somewhere ahead and uphill. Amos turned for better protection into a place where the trees stood close-spaced in a virgin stand.

Now there was not a sound. Henry looked at his friend and rolled his eyes. "They'll be scattered all over hell, comin' down this way. Isn't any way we can make it back down yonder by staying' on the far side of that creek with the willows between us an' them, without them tracking' us all the way."

Amos agreed in silence. He nodded his head, twisted to

look apprehensively back up through the semidarkness, then led off again, this time northward, parallel to the creek but quite a few hundred yards from it.

The sun had topped its zenith and was beginning to slide across a flawless turquoise western sky in the direction of peaks so distant and hazy they appeared as crumpled brown paper.

Amos did not stop until they reached the creek, even though he was breathing like a bellows and they were at least a mile from where the watercourse curled around through the uplands before beginning its dogleg run southward toward the settler camp.

Where he exhaustedly stopped there was a scattered jumble of glass rock where Indians from earlier times had set up camps for months on end to make arrowheads. The glass rock was pure obsidian. There was abundant evidence of early tribes camping here: ancient fire rings, barely discernible circular sunken places, fire-blackened bones of very large animals, ancient moccasin paths worn into solid rock.

Amos ignored everything but their back-trail. "They'll track us this far"—he gestured—"but not over the glass rock. We can maybe cross the glass-rock field, then double back an' get into them willows along the creek. By then, it ought to be dark enough for us to get all the way back to that damned settler camp."

CHAPTER 12
Toward Day's End

Henry was apprehensive because the field of glass rock was at least a hundred yards across without a single standing tree or a decent clump of underbrush to be used for concealment if their angry pursuers got close enough to see them running.

Amos did not look back. Henry could hear his lungs sucking in great amounts of air and blowing it out, but he knew better than to admonish his old friend to go a little slower.

Amos went down into a swale, and when Henry reached him he was flat on his back, looking straight up and making wind-broke noises like a horse. Henry flattened along the brim to look back.

They were back there, quartering like coon dogs. It looked like maybe seven or eight of them. He put his chin on the ground, watching. Below him Amos's breathing did not seem to be any easier.

Every man over yonder on the east side of the field of glass rock was carrying either a rifle or a carbine. Henry and Amos had belt guns and knives.

Salty sweat ran into Henry's eyes, stinging them; he raised a sleeve to wipe away the perspiration. There were four points of the compass; those sign-hunting pursuers could go in any one of them. That made the odds against their choosing the correct direction three to one. Henry let go a noisy sigh about that. Then he reminded himself that Fate, or whoever handled things like this, was as likely to be asleep on tanned hides in his cabin as he was to be looking out for a pair of sinewy old leathery-hided miscreants who were, Henry emphasized to himself, too old for this kind of damned foolishness.

They turned back eastward into the trees at a dogtrot and disappeared from Henry's view. He let his whole body sag. Below him Amos coughed, sat up, craned around, and said, "Are you crazy? This ain't no time to sleep. Where are they?"

"Went back," muttered Henry, mouth against the earth.

"Back eastward?"

Henry pushed himself around with an effort. "Yes, back eastward. Get up."

They had to walk southward in a crouch so as not to be visible above the lip of the shallow arroyo. Henry did not believe anyone would be watching from the far side of the field of glass rock, but he stayed crouched anyway.

Thirst bothered them, especially when their arroyo eased eastward on a long-running angle until they could hear Coffee Creek.

It was hot, despite the occasional ground-hugging breeze that came bumbling up their arroyo. Amos held the lead until the ground underfoot became soft, then he halted, raised up without his hat, and peered around like a marmot, shoulders corkscrewing and head swiveling. He said, "Not a sign."

Henry pushed up and belly-crawled into the willows on the west side of the creek, ignored a snake that had been drinking, pushed his head completely beneath the water, and came up snorting. The snake sucked back, lidless eyes fixed in what must have been total astonishment. Henry was probably the largest thing the snake had ever seen crawl up on its belly to drink.

Amos did not crawl the short intervening distance, but he did not approach the creek in an erect stance either. He too saw the snake, but his reaction was different; he pushed out a stiff leg, got a boot toe in the mud under the snake, and kicked hard. The snake fell into the grass two yards away, got righted, and did not once look back as it sashayed out of sight.

Henry used his disreputable hat to scoop water and up-end it above his head. When he was soaked and that little vagrant breeze came up from the south to cool him through evaporation, he remembered something and felt frantically for his little pipe. It was still in his pocket. He was relieved as he faced his old friend.

"My guess is that they gave up on us and went back around the lower side of the slope to be in position when darkness comes."

For a while Amos did not answer. He stood up and looked down the creek at the willows, which were on both sides for miles, with only an occasional open place. "It'd do my heart real good to figure you was right, Henry. But over a lot of years I've seen you come up wrong so many times I'm half afraid to move for fear them bastards is over there watchin' for movement. Get up. You look like a drowned rat. Let's make some more tracks."

It seemed to take them longer to get back down opposite the wagon camp than it had taken them to depart from it. They halted several times to splash across the watercourse, gently part the spindly willows, and look around.

There was no one in sight to the west, but there probably wouldn't have been anyway; it was dark where the forest began and continued to be that way up the eastern slope as far as they could see. To be seen at that distance, someone over there would have to be moving.

Henry led off to the south. The heat wasn't as strong among the lacy willows, but there was something just as annoying: mosquitoes in droves.

They heard someone using an axe, which was encouraging. When they halted again a short while later, Henry wrinkled his nose. "Supper fire," he stated, and moved along until they crossed a gravelly, shallow place that had evidently been cleared of growth so that vehicles could cross there.

This place was only a few hundred yards from the area where they had halted after sprinting from the camp much earlier in the day.

Finally Henry stopped, waded the creek with Amos close behind, pushed clear of the willows, and stood in sunlight gazing across the open area toward the wagons.

Amos tipped his hat and ranged a searching glance along the farther-off timbered slope to the left of the camp. He didn't have to see anyone up there; he knew in his bones they were watching and waiting, probably mad as hornets about having been set afoot, which would make them more determined than ever to raid the settlers. For their horses, among other things.

Henry said, "It'd sure help if there was a big flash of blue lightning over yonder, wouldn't it?"

Amos grunted. The sky was absolutely flawless. He gauged the distance as he had done earlier and began to expand and empty his lungs for the race toward shelter.

"We could sit for a couple of hours, wait for the sun to go down," Henry suggested.

Amos fished for his twist and worried off a cud before replying. "More likely three hours." He spat. "They ain't done anythin' about fillin' the water barrels."

Henry looked around, scowling. "How? The old man's riders would pick them off like crows on a fence."

Amos chewed, hunkered down, and remained silent.

Henry sighed as he also squatted. "You ready?" he asked.

"Ready as I'll ever be, but when we run over here this morning I'm here to tell you m'legs felt like they was turnin' to punk. How far'd you say that was?"

Henry squinted at the distant wagons. There were people moving, smoke rising from the stone ring, animals wandering in search of something to eat. He had never been good at estimating distances except in miles, and that camp was a hell of a lot less than even one mile. "About as far as a good horse could jump out in a few minutes," he said.

Amos seemed satisfied with that. He jettisoned his chew, stood up, hitched at his belt, and reset his hat.

Henry unwound too, but all he did was yank his old hat down hard and stare at a place between two wagons where a tongue from one rig had been run beneath the belly of the other. He had jumped that wagon tongue this morning on his way to the creek. Now he would be satisfied if he could just reach the damned thing.

Amos grunted and broke free of willows and shadows. His racing gait was thunderous and physically straining. Henry could have left him well to the rear if he had not elected to run beside him.

They had gotten almost halfway when someone up ahead among the wagons whistled loudly. People flitted, raising dust in the compound. Women and children filtered past the men, who were hurrying in the direction the sentry standing on a tailgate was pointing.

Guns bristled. Amos was sucking air like a fish out of water, and he gasped out a sizzling swearword. Henry began to wave his old hat wildly.

No one fired as the runners crossed the halfway mark. Several settlers stepped over the wagon tongue and walked forward a short distance, yelling encouragement. Amos's eyes were bulging. He had done more running today than he had done in a very long while. He was not built for this, but above everything else he'd often said that the reason menfolk did not have to climb or run hard was because God had given humans two legs and a fairly large brain, and had given horses four legs and a little tiny brain, therefore horses were equipped to climb and run when men told them to.

Henry said, "Gettin' there."

Amos did not even turn his head. Henry couldn't have heard him anyway; all the settlers were shouting encouragment now. Amos turned bloodshot eyes in the direction of the distant dark slope, saw the tiny puff of soiled white smoke, and gave Henry a furious blow and fell with him.

The muzzle blast did not reach the settlers, suddenly silenced by what Amos had done, until both the squaw men were on the ground. Then it arrived, clear as a bell.

Several settlers turned back across the clearing with their rifles.

Henry regained his feet, glared at Amos, who was slower rising, and covered the final hundred yards by himself. When Amos came up moments later, blowing like a steam engine, Henry was leaning on a wagon with people crowding around, some offering canteens, some offering rags to mop the sweat off with, some excitedly talking. Old man Fulbright was farther back, sitting on a tailgate and swinging his legs, for all the world like a wizened, nut-brown elf covered with face feathers. He was hugging a burlap-wrapped jug on his shady side.

Unsmiling, gaunt Luther Davis helped Amos ease down on the wagon tongue. "You done right well for a man your age," he said, and as Amos looked up a woman in a bonnet who had more tact smiled at Amos. "For any age, Mister Cardiff. You ran like a deer."

Hugh Morton shouldered through. "We didn't miss you for a while," he stated, eyeing them both. "Someone said maybe you fellers had decided to skip out before the fight."

Henry was finally breathing easier, so he said, "Mister Morton, point out the man who said that."

The wagon boss reddened a little. "Don't recollect who it was, Mister Potter."

Henry was not placated. He looked around and gestured. "Ladies, I'd take it kindly if you'd walk off a ways . . . please."

The older women nudged the younger ones. When only men were left, Henry fixed big Hugh Morton with an un-blinking stare. He pulled out his big belt knife, eased it down into the front waistband of his britches, and said, "I don't think anyone said that to you, Mister Morton. I think you just made it up. And if you did, you are a lyin' son of a bitch . . . Me'n Amos used that earlier commotion to reach the creek. We went up into the damned timber, found Tenkiller's horses, and run them off, settin' him and his stronghearts afoot. If they figured to ride over here after dark and maybe ride away afterward, now they got to do it all on foot, and I can tell you from experience, raiders don't do nothin' on foot to people who got horses to run them down with."

Morton stood big and lowering, but it was Luther Davis who spoke next. "We owe you gents, Mister Potter. Hugh didn't mean anything."

Henry pushed through, stepped over the tongue where Amos was sitting, and kept on walking until he had reached the stone ring, where Sun Sister and her new friend got him a huge dish of food.

Amos sat awhile, until most of the men had drifted away, then arose, bowed his back a little, and smiled at the wagon boss. "This here is your lucky day," he said. "One more word out of you and he'd have opened you up like a chicken and you'd have been carryin' your guts around in a bucket . . . Mister Fulbright, that ain't French toilet water in that jug, is it?"

Davis waited until Amos departed with old Fulbright, then gave Hugh Morton a rough slap on the shoulder as he said, "In my time, where I come from, I've known a lot of men like them two. Real careful about givin' offense and damned quick to take offense. They aren't like the rest of us, Hugh."

Morton shook his head and started away with Davis at his side. They did not even look in the direction of the fire ring as they passed by; they stopped near the barrel barricade, where several men were leaning on rifles squinting northeast in the direction of the distant timbered slope.

"Any sign?" he asked.

"Nothing," a rifleman growled, and canted his head at the sky. "Be dusk before too long, Mister Morton."

Luther Davis went back to the stone ring for some hot coffee and cast a sidelong glance at Henry, whose knife was back in its belt sheath. "You think they won't attack tonight, Mister Potter?"

Henry had to swallow hard before he could reply. "I got no idea. I know they'll go after their horses, and that might use up what's left of the daylight. Maybe well into the night as well, if them horses head back up to the meadow."

"Then we might get through until tomorrow?" Davis asked, holding the tin cup without raising it, his eyes fixed on Henry.

"Yup. Might."

Sun Sister came over to lean down and speak softly to Henry. "I don't know what it is, but I think Ned wants that wounded man to die."

Henry's eyes popped wide open. He almost dropped his dish as he stood up looking out past the barrel barricade. The handsome horse was out there, but the man wasn't. He turned back. "Him, Sun Sister?"

"Yes." She jutted her jaw in the direction of the widow Henderson's wagon. "Over there."

"How the hell did he get from out there in here?"

"When the men in here were firing into the trees, three other women went with me. We carried him back."

Henry paled. "What in hell was you thinking of? He could have been dead, Sun Sister."

"I could see him trying to crawl. Henry, Ned is in the wagon with him. He is very mad."

"What about?"

"I don't know. He won't let anyone into the wagon."

Henry handed her his plate, looked around for Amos, saw him sprawled in late-day shadows with Ben Fulbright with the croaker-sacked jug between them, and stamped over. He leaned and rapped Amos on the shoulder. "Come with me. No damned questions, just get up off your backside."

Amos stared, but eventually pushed up with the help of

the wagon spokes at his back. He ran the back of one hand across his sweat-sticky stubbly face and jerked his head for Henry to lead the way.

Behind him, the widow Henderson came around from somewhere beyond her wagon to stand, hands on hips, looking after them as Ben Fulbright unconsciously ran bent fingers through his beard. "That other one's sure on the peck today," he said. "Look at him over there, talkin' a mile a minute and wavin' his arms." Fulbright scrambled up to his feet as Amos and Henry started back toward the wagon. He moved closer to the buxom widow Henderson, presumably to protect her if the need arose, but possibly so that she could protect him, since she was taller, heavier, and more muscular in appearance.

CHAPTER 13
A Man Named Butler

Amos addressed the robustly handsome woman. "We'd like a word with the gent in your wagon, if you got no objection, Miz Henderson."

Her reply was polite. "He told me when they carried the wounded man in there that he didn't want to be disturbed, Mister Cardiff." She paused without blinking in her regard of Amos. "But if you'd like, I'll climb up and ask if he'll see you gentlemen."

Old Amos was at his raffish best during this interlude. He had been powerfully attracted to the woman since his first sighting of her. He now smiled warmly at her as he spoke. "No need for you to do that. Henry'n I can climb up there. And if Mister Travis don't want to see nobody, why we'll just climb back down. But it was real decent of you to make the offer. I know a real lady when I see one, Miz Henderson."

Old Fulbright and Henry were both staring at Amos. He seemed either unaware of or totally indifferent to this as he lifted his hat, made a very slight but unmistakable bow, and moved past in the direction of the front-wheel hub.

Henry pushed up and whispered, "You wheedlin' fraud, Amos."

Ben Fulbright, on the other hand, stood with Amelia Henderson, watching them swarm up to the high seat behind which wagon canvas hung slackly open. "You got an admirer, Amelia. A genuine leather-shirted squaw man."

She waited until Amos and Henry were out of sight

through the opening behind the driver's seat, then took old Fulbright by the arm and briskly hiked him away from the wagon before stopping to release his arm and glare. "You are ungrateful for what they did for us, Mister Fulbright, and I don't like that. Mister Cardiff is a gallant individual."

Old Fulbright agreed instantly, his tiny blue eyes glowing with warmth. "He is that for a fact, Amelia, and folks owe him and his friend. I just meant—"

"Go see what the men are discussing at the fire ring and don't come back until the gentlemen in there with Mister Travis come out."

It would be a very long wait, because the men in the Henderson wagon, which was stuffy, ten degrees warmer than it was outside, and burdened with the things settlers hauled along to place in their new homes somewhere, had barely enough room to squat. Some of that room was taken up by the pallet of blankets and flannel sheets the widow Henderson had organized for the man with ashen lips, pale coloring, and dry-appearing eyes who was lying on it.

Ned Travis's face was shiny from sweat as he watched Amos and Henry work their way from the front of the wagon, with its eerie gray-white light, toward the rear, where Travis was sitting on a small stool. He said nothing, but his facial expression was hostile.

The man on the pallet had a sticky bandage around his lower middle where someone had poulticed the wound. His breathing was in deep inward sweeps followed by exhalations, then agonizingly long moments before he struggled to take down another big breath.

He was about Travis's age and build, lean and lanky. He had light hair, somewhere between ash-blond and roan. He watched the pair of older men approach with a languid gaze.

As Amos settled on the floorboards he let his breath out slowly and silently. It had to be nothing short of a miracle that the man with the roan hair was still alive. He had been shot in the morning and it was now close to dusk.

Henry did not take his eyes off the stranger as he asked Ned about the man's wound. The reply was brusque. "If it'd been a lead bullet he'd have been stiff as a ramrod by now. It was one of them steel-jacketed bullets. Passed through his guts somewhere and went out the back. Not much of a hole either way, but the bleedin' don't stop. A trickle, but it don't stop. Sun Sister and the woman who owns this wagon tried their skills. Didn't seem to help much. What do you two want?"

Henry smiled at the dying man as he replied. "Came along to see if we could help any."

"You can't. Is that all you want?"

Henry finally looked at Sun Sister's man. "Who is he? Why did he come here—or try to come here? Didn't he know these folks was under siege?"

Ned was not his customary calm, unruffled self. He glared at Henry. "How in hell would he know? He was just ridin' out there, saw the camp, and decided to come over."

Amos saw the dying man's pale eyes rise to Ned's face and remain there.

Henry asked again who the stranger was, and Ned answered curtly, "Fred Butler. He runs a shop over in Bent's Siding."

Henry gazed at Butler. "What kind of shop?"

Ned answered again. "Deals in chemicals and such like."

Butler's eyes were still on Ned, motionless, tired looking.

Amos leaned around his partner to ask Ned Travis a question. "You knew him before today, Ned?"

This time Henry saw Fred Butler's eyes flicker, but the man still made no attempt to speak as Ned cleared his throat. "We met. When I saw him ridin' toward the wagons this morning I remembered meetin' him before."

The wounded man ran his tongue sluggishly around parched lips and finally spoke in a weary tone of voice that faded softly. "I brought him . . . the money." There was a long pause while Butler went through his difficult breathing process, then two more words. "I knew . . ."

Ned's shoulders hunched as he stared at the dying man. The conversation of a couple of men walking past reached inside the wagon very clearly: they were talking about water; the barrels were nearly empty. One man thought they could get through the night with possibly enough water left for the next day if they were careful.

Inside the wagon there was not a sound. Amos leaned forward, placed two fingers on the side of Fred Butler's throat, held them there for a long moment, then removed them and eased back. "He's dead."

They sat in motionless silence and gazed at the bluish lips, ashen face, and drying eyes until Henry moved enough to face Ned Travis. Henry was thinking back to that surreptitious meeting at the horse corral out behind Ned's cabin. Fred Butler had the build of that elusive silhouette Henry had seen that night.

Henry broke the silence. "What did he know, Ned?"

Ned was still looking bitterly at the dead man and did not reply until Henry reached and shook him a little. "What did he know? You heard him. He said he knew something."

Ned shook off Henry's hand and answered angrily. "How the hell do I know what he meant? He knew . . . he could have known anything."

He started to gather himself to rise.

Amos stood up first, filling the narrow space, blocking it very effectively. "What money, Ned? He said he brought you the money."

Ned's aggravation did not prevent him from being able to answer carefully. "He didn't say *me*, Amos. He said he brought *him* money. I got no idea who he meant. Maybe one of the settlers."

Henry also rose. Now there was barely enough room for them to stand. There was certainly not enough room for one of them to depart unless the two men nearest the front of the wagon moved in that direction first.

Behind Ned the tailgate was up and chained into place, and the canvas had been pulled nearly closed with the pucker string tied at the bottom. The hole in the center of the closed canvas was barely large enough for a man to put his head through.

Henry was closest to Ned, but even though Amos was behind Henry, he was still close enough to reach around his friend.

"He didn't give you no money, Ned?" Amos said.

"No! I told you, he didn't say he gave me any money. Amos, he was driftin' in an' out of consciousness all day. Worse this afternoon. For the last hour or so he hadn't talked at all."

Henry looked down. "Took him a long time to die, didn't it? What sticks in my craw, Ned, is you not allowin' anyone in here."

Ned glared. "You two come in, didn't you?"

"Sure did. Just climbed in. But that lady who owns the wagon told us you didn't want no one in here."

"Well for chrissake, a dyin' person don't need a lot of people crowdin' around and staring, does he?"

Henry agreed with that. "Nope, he don't. Maybe if they'd crowded in before he got too weak, he would have told them somethin' you didn't want anyone to hear." As Henry's head came up and his eyes met the hostile gaze of Ned Travis, he said something else. "I've known you a long time, Ned. We've hunted and scouted together. Even been on raids together and this is the first time I ever saw you sweatin' like this and nervous as a cornered lion."

Ned's color darkened; sweat trickled at his temples. He looked from one man to the other and finally said, "Move up front, Amos. Henry and I'll follow. It's hard to breathe in here. We can talk outside." He gestured with his left hand for Amos to move. Amos might have turned, but when

Henry didn't, did not even take his eyes off Ned's face, Amos remained in place.

A right-handed man gestured with his right hand, not his left hand. Unless he had something in mind that required the use of his right hand. Henry's suspicions were getting more solid by the moment. He arrived at a decision but could not implement it when he was less than four feet from Ned Travis. Even if Henry could beat Ned at drawing, cocking, and firing his belt gun—which was not very likely because Ned was much younger and quicker, and by now was poised and tensed—if there was a gunfight at that distance neither of them would leave the widow Henderson's wagon alive.

Henry said, "Take your pants down, Ned."

Ned's eyes sprang wide open, flabbergasted, and that was when Henry swung, bringing his knotty old scarred set of knuckles up from the area of his hip while twisting his entire body into the strike.

Amos was too surprised to breathe as he heard the sound of bone against bone and Ned Travis went backward, striking a dresser. Ned hung there a second, then jackknifed forward and fell facedown across the dead man's pallet.

Amos let his breath out as Henry's lips moved in profanity while he held his right fist against his chest with his left hand. "I broke it," he gasped. "Broke m'goddamn hand, Amos. Here . . . squeeze past me and yank down his britches and pull up his huntin' shirt."

Amos started to obey, then checked himself and looked around in bafflement. "What for?"

Henry swore and started to shoulder past to do it himself, but Amos growled at him. "All right. All right. Mind your damned hand and get out of the way."

Amos worked first at pushing Ned off the dead man, then drew his knife and sliced through a leather belt, grasped Travis's trousers at the ankles, leaned back, and pulled.

He straightened up wide-eyed as Henry crowed exultantly,

"Naw, Butler didn't mean him, the lyin' bastard. Pull up his shirt and unbuckle that money belt."

Amos obeyed without a sound. When he finally straightened up with the belt across his palm he hefted it and rolled his eyes. "It's chock-full, Henry. Paper bills ain't supposed to have any weight, but they sure do this time. Here, heft it."

Henry was still cradling his injured hand. "Put it over my shoulder," he told his partner, "and tie that son of a bitch so's he can't wiggle a toe. And cram somethin' into his mouth."

Amos worked with sweat flowing until it nearly blinded him and he had to pause to mop it off. The unconscious man had been trussed by someone who knew every way to lash game to horses and tie every kind of knot, including knots that tightened themselves as strain was put upon them.

When they climbed down out of the wagon Hugh Morton was addressing the assembled settlers over at the fire ring. Amos led the way to the far side of the Henderson wagon and away to the concealment of other wagons and barricades.

Henry followed, thick money belt draped over one shoulder, cradling his injured right hand against his chest.

Daylight was waning. The forested uplands looked darker than ever, more menacing and forbidding. Elsewhere in open country, daylight was taking on the russet, yellow, red, and bronze shades of autumn even though it was still summertime.

CHAPTER 14
Toward Darkness

Amos peered beneath a wagon and saw crates and small articles of furniture put there by a settler family to have more room in their wagon. He got down and crawled.

Henry did the same, but had a harder time of it because of his throbbing right hand. When Amos stopped crawling and squared around with his back against a wooden box, Henry tossed him the money belt with his left hand.

Neither of them said a word. Beyond, in the direction of the fire ring, Hugh Morton was addressing the assembled settlers, his words carrying easily to the men beneath the wagon. He was telling them of the danger, outlining their position—which was not enviable, as they already knew—and detailing individual men to particular points inside the surround.

Neither of the squaw men beneath the wagon paid any attention. Amos was very painstakingly smoothing out greenbacks and placing them on the ground, and Henry, no longer cradling his swelling right hand, sat there with his eyes getting wider by the moment.

Amos finally leaned back and said, "Three thousand dollars. I never in all my life seen that much money in one pile, did you?"

Henry hadn't. "Not even half that much. I wish to hell Butler hadn't died. Amos, remember me tellin' you about Ned sneakin' around in the night to meet someone? Remember how we tracked him to where he left his horse? Well, I'd stake my outfit that was Butler."

Amos leaned to gently smooth some crumpled greenbacks. As he finished doing this he raised his eyes to his partner. "Aren't no answers unless Ned gives 'em."

Someone called from the center of the compound and repeated the call. The words were indistinguishable to the men crouching beneath the wagon, but the tone echoed alarm.

Henry turned to crawl out. Behind him, Amos grabbed up the greenbacks and stuffed them haphazardly into the money belt. Looking hastily around, he found a raised binder-block, shoved the belt in, and scrambled quickly out on the west side of the wagon, where Henry was waiting.

There was noisy activity around front. Amos peered around and across the open country toward the timbered slope, but dusk was steadily settling; visibility was about three or four hundred feet and no farther. Those sloping uplands were several times that distant.

A man's shout rose above other sounds. "Watch close, you'll see them."

Henry and Amos walked around the wagon and stopped where men with weapons, as well as a few armed women, were craning beyond the barricade in the direction the sentry on a tailgate was pointing.

Henry did not see anything out there. "What's he pointing at?"

Amos grunted. "Most likely nothing. Daylight's passing. It's been a long wait and they're nervous. We better go see about Ned before the widow-woman or old Fulbright finds him."

As they turned southward Henry raised his swollen hand and gingerly flexed the joints. Amos saw this from the corner of his eye and said, "It's not broke, it just feels like it."

Henry continued to work the hand as they approached the

widow Henderson's wagon. "We better find some chain," he murmured.

Amos was reaching for the wheel hub when he replied. "This isn't a good time to talk to Morton about Ned. Him and the others see renegades every time a horse casts a shadow."

They climbed into the wagon, which was full of ghostly grayness, bumped their way noisily toward the tailgate, and stopped where the dead man's pallet blocked further progress. Ned Travis rolled over and looked at them. He growled something through the gag and Amos made a little clucking sound. "You'd ought to watch your language. This here wagon belongs to a lady."

Ned strained at the bindings and growled again. Amos leaned down, removed the gag, and cautioned him about making a lot of noise.

"Where's my money belt?" Ned snarled.

Amos responded laconically while squatting a few feet from him. "It's hid. Ned, if you want to get loose, tell us how's it come you had three thousand dollars."

Ned sat perfectly still, looking steadily at them. He made no attempt to reply, so Amos wagged his head, leaned, and in an almost casual manner, swung his open palm. The blow toppled Ned, and although he struggled to get up again, he was unable to do so until Amos grabbed his shirtfront and pulled him up.

Henry offered a suggestion to the younger man. "There's one dead man in here and another one won't make things much worse. Besides, the settlers is runnin' around like a bunch of chickens, seein' enemies everywhere. We can pitch you out of here, drag you off a ways, and slit your throat. If you squawk or yell, we can do it right here. Ned, if I was in your boots, tied like a shoat and all, I'd try to get along. We're goin' to find out about that money one way or another. I'm givin' you good advice."

Ned's mouth remained closed; his cheek where he had

been slapped felt hot. He had known the two older men for a long time. He had also heard how they had sneaked up yonder and set Tenkiller's raiders on foot. He finally spoke. "They're coming. You know what Plume and the old man will do to you for runnin' off their horses?"

Henry nodded solemnly. "Yeah, we know. You want to know somethin' else? You won't be around to see it."

Amos cocked his head as some hurrying people went past, drew his knife, and leaned for the thrust. Ned bleated, but evidently none of the settlers outside the wagon heard him, and he did that only once because the tip of Amos's knife was sticking in his throat. "Not another sound," Amos warned Ned, then lowered the knife until the tip was directly in front of Ned Travis's soft parts.

"The money," he said. "Ned, so help me I'll do it. *The money!*"

Ned spoke fiercely but quietly. "North of the camp . . . I hunted up there . . ."

"Goddammit, we know that. You was up there a lot. Get on with it."

Ned turned crafty. "Turn me loose and give me an hour's head start and I'll tell you."

Henry's patience was thin. He leaned over his partner's shoulder and said, "Stick the son of a bitch!"

Amos's arm was moving when Ned sucked back his body and spilled out words. "I found a vein of gold up there. Half as thick as a man's wrist. I pouched some of it and waited until it was time to go to Bent's Siding for supplies. I told Tenkiller I'd take my horses and pack back what we needed . . . I showed the gold to Butler. We worked it out so's we'd meet at night—he'd give me the money and I'd give him another pouch . . . That's where the three thousand dollars come from."

Ned eased back, staring. Henry blew out a noisy breath. When his surprise had passed, Henry wanted to know how Butler had known Ned would be at the settler camp. Ned's answer was short. "Last time we met was behind the cabin at my corral. I told him about the settlers at Coffee Creek. I told him there was goin' to be a raid on 'em, and that I'd try to reach them before the raid if I could . . . and you two gave me the best way to do it I could have got when you turned their scout loose. That's why I helped you when Plume came to the Mexican's cabin. To have a couple more guns along in case Plume came after me. I was goin' to run for it anyway in the night, but this way it looked better and you two was in it up to your hocks when you braced Plume. A man's got to be quick about recognizing opportunities and takin' advantage of them."

Amos asked a question. "What did Butler mean when he said he knew?"

"I just told you, damn it. He knew I'd be with these wagon people. He knew I'd have another pouch for him and he knew to bring the money for the last pouch . . . What the hell is goin' on out there?"

Several men were shouting, and the loose animals inside the compound were moving in fright. Henry worked his way back toward the front of the wagon, stepped across the seat, and saw people dipping buckets into barrels and handing them along to a man who was trying to douse a canvas fire. As Henry watched, the fire flickered out.

He turned back. "Gag him, Amos, and come out here."

Ned swung his head as Amos leaned over with the gag. Amos growled and Ned stopped moving. He tried to speak, but with the gag tied in place the sound was guttural. Amos wagged a finger. "Don't do nothing silly, Ned," he cautioned, and went bumping his way up front to climb down to where Henry was standing. The widow Henderson approached them, ignoring Henry to address Amos. "They are sneaking closer," she said, gesturing. "I need my husband's rifle."

Amos blocked her path. "Henry'll get it."

"He don't know where—"

"He'll find it, ma'am, won't you, Henry." As Henry turned

to climb back up into the wagon, Amos said, "Ma'am, there's a dead man in there. He's not a pretty sight."

"He may be the luckiest one of us, Mister Cardiff, before this night is over."

Amos's reply was placating. "Naw. Don't think like that. Me and Henry will figure something out. Where did the fire bundle come from?"

She pointed. "Not from the northeast where we were watching. It came from the west, from the direction of the creek where you and Mister Potter were earlier." She dropped her arm as Henry came down the side of the wagon, carrying a long-barreled rifle and a belt of bullets for it. "They are all around us, Mister Cardiff. Ben said it's exactly like an Indian attack."

As Henry passed over the weapon and ammunition, Amos smiled at the buxom woman. "You be careful with that thing, ma'am, and don't get in front of no light."

She watched them walk over to Hugh Morton, who was talking to Luther Davis. When they came up, the settlers stopped talking and gazed at them until Henry said, "Might be better if everyone wasn't on this side, Mister Morton." Before the wagon boss could reply Henry continued, "By my figurin', you got more men than they have."

Luther scowled. "How do you know that?"

Henry smiled at the scowl. "Because even with old Tenkiller along, Plume don't have more'n maybe six or eight stronghearts, and you got about ten or twelve men and some big lads."

Amos, who had been stuffing his face with molasses-cured, spat first, then spoke. "Plume might not have that many. Some of 'em may have gone back for the horses."

Luther shook his head. "They was yonder in the trees on the east side. Now there's some of 'em on the west side. That's a surround, Mister Cardiff."

Amos spat again before replying. "All right. You stay in

here and keep close watch. Henry and I'll go out yonder and see what we can flush out."

Morton's face cleared. "Take Luther here with you. There's a couple other—"

"All right," Amos interrupted. "Luther, but no more. It's pretty easy to get killed by mistake in the dark. And it'd help if you'd keep an eye on your shooters, because when we're out there, maybe tryin' to get back, I'd take it real personal if someone fired at me from here."

Morton would have spoken again, but Henry spoke first. "One thing a man can count on in a mess like this, Mister Morton, is that hidin' behind barrels and wagons, waitin' for targets, don't do nearly as much good as takin' the fight out yonder to the attackers."

Morton said, "You don't have rifles."

Henry replied, "Most times I been in this kind of a fix, a rifle's a damned burden. If there's any shootin' in the dark it's not goin' to be at rifle distance." He nodded at Luther Davis's long-gun. "Leave it here. Make sure that belt gun is loaded. It'd help if you had a knife, but waitin' for you to get one would be wastin' time. You ready, Mister Davis?"

Morton accepted the Kentucky rifle as Luther nodded at Henry. His expression was uncertain but dogged.

As Amos led off toward the west side, he paused to say one more thing to Hugh Morton. "That feller in the lady's wagon is dead. The feller we brought with us named Travis is in there with him, tied and gagged. We'd take it kindly if you folks didn't untie him."

Morton's eyes widened, but Amos was moving briskly away, followed by his partner and the gaunt man. Several settlers approached Hugh Morton, but said nothing as they watched Amos and Henry move beyond the wagons. Morton, though, finally found his voice. "You boys keep sharp watch here. I'm going down to the Henderson wagon."

One of the other men spoke up, his voice reedy. "It might help if I was to go out there with them, Mister Morton."

The big man looked around. "They don't want anyone but Luther with them, Ben."

"I've done my share of skulkin' before, Mister Morton."

"I know you have, Mister Fulbright, but they said plain as day they didn't want any more of us to go out there with them."

The discussion might have continued—old Ben Fulbright was a very stubborn individual—but at the lower end of the compound voices were raised as a fire bundle came soaring, doubly bright against the night sky.

Its trajectory was a high curving arc from the west. But this time the thrower had either misjudged the distance to a wagon-top or hurled his torch with greater force than was needed. The bundle landed out in the compound, burning fiercely as only pitch can burn.

A settler bawled for men to bring shovels and smother the thing with dirt, to save the water.

CHAPTER 15
A Wagon Tongue

Henry scouted ahead of Amos and Luther Davis until he could look over his shoulder and see the eerie-looking wagons a fair distance back. He halted, sank to one knee, waited until his companions arrived, and gestured for Amos to go northwesterly while Luther Davis went in the opposite direction. He did not have to warn Amos, but he warned Luther.

"Don't shoot if you come onto someone until you're damned certain it isn't me or Amos. It'd be better if you didn't shoot at all—try stalkin' from the rear and knockin' them over the head. After the first gunshot they'll know we're out here. You ready?"

Luther nodded, and Henry told him to crawl. Henry and Amos watched the gaunt man move away. Amos wagged his head, but refrained from commenting until Luther was lost in the gloom, then he said, "It couldn't be a surround. Plume don't have that many raiders."

Henry's reply was dry. "How'd these people ever get this far? Of course it wasn't no surround. Plume had 'em do somethin' to make the settlers all stand over on the east side while someone crept around here to toss them bundles."

Henry gestured and Amos moved warily away. Henry waited a long while, listening, trying to imagine where those fire bundles had come from. He was about to move ahead when something attracted his attention to the left.

From the wagons it would not have been possible to see it, but Henry was far enough westward so that even though the

111

sputtering fire was being shielded as someone used a sulphur match to light a fire bundle, Henry could make out the flash. He turned toward it, moving swiftly. The distance appeared to be about a hundred yards southward, and although he could have used his belt gun he did not pause in his crab-crawl to draw it. One gunshot out here would destroy their purpose.

He did not believe he would be able to reach the man in time, and he was correct. The darkly smoking, fiercely burning wad of pitch rose out of the darkness and made a high arc as it tumbled end over end in the direction of the wagons.

Henry risked getting to his feet to move more swiftly in a crouching run. He heard people yelling in the distance as they saw the burning torch coming, but he ignored that to concentrate on the location of the thrower.

A man arose from the ground on Henry's right, north of the raider. Henry dropped and rolled, sure he had been seen. He heard a loud grunt and stopped to raise up. The man he had seen on his right was no longer in sight, but dead ahead there was a thrashing sound. He jumped up, drew the belt knife, and hastened forward.

They were struggling on the ground, Luther and a thicker, unkempt man whose hat had been knocked off. The man was locked in Luther's arms, struggling to break free. Luther was clinging desperately, evidently aware that he had attacked a man for whom he was no match.

The thick man had his belt knife clear of its sheath, but he could not use it because his arms were pinned to his sides. Henry stopped, saw their faces, dropped to one knee, and pushed his six-gun within inches of Mullins's face. He cocked the gun and said, "Drop the knife, Andy."

Luther relinquished his hold and got unsteadily to his feet. "I should have shot him," he said, panting.

Henry eased down his gun hammer as he said, "I'm glad you didn't." He holstered the weapon and pushed Mullins down in the trampled grass. "Who's out here with you?" he asked. When Mullins did not respond, Henry slapped the man hard with his open hand, then drew his knife. "Andy, for the last time, who is out here with you?"

Mullins's reply was low and angry. "They're goin' to skin you alive, Henry. The old man was fit to be tied when he found out what you'd done at the camp. If he never does anything else, he's goin' to—"

Henry's open hand moved too fast for Mullins to see it coming in the gloom. The sound was sharp. This time Mullins nearly fell sideways under the impact. As he righted himself he raised a hand to his face.

"Who is out here with you? Andy, I'm goin' to open you up like a bear—"

"There was two—that kid you made a fool out of by runnin' off the horses he was supposed to be minding and that 'breed who used to partner around with the Mexican. Ruffy Barton. I sent them on to Plume because they wasn't fellers I wanted behind me in this. Anyway, don't take but one man to set wagons afire."

As he finished speaking, Mullins peered venomously at Luther Davis. "I'd have killed him, Henry. He ain't no match for me and never would be. I thought at first it was Amos or you, but he didn't have the strength nor the heft of you fellers. Where is Amos?"

Henry ignored the question. "We're goin' to take you back with us, Andy." Henry tossed Mullins's knife away, handed his six-gun to Luther Davis, who was still panting, then yanked Mullins to his feet and started him with a shove. "Out ahead, Andy. I never feel real good about walkin' up to wagon camps in the dark when everyone's orry-eyed, watchin' for shadows to shoot at."

Mullins's voice rose in pitch as he said, "Call out to 'em, for chrissake."

"Shut up and keep moving!"

Luther walked slightly behind them and to one side. He was still a little breathless. He was also resentful about not being allowed to use his weapon, and now if their prisoner was telling the truth about being out there alone, a gunshot would not have made any difference.

"Henry?"

"What."

"Is Ned up there too?"

"Yeah. Him and Sun Sister. Andy, how many men's Plume got?"

"Tenkiller's with 'em. Countin' him and Plume, there's nine."

"Eight without you?"

"Yeah." Mullins was quiet as he watched the wagons materialize out of the darkness. But when they could make out details of the settler compound he said, "You goin' to keep 'em off me, Henry?"

"No."

Mullins bleated again. "All I done was what I was told to do. Except for landin' one of the fire-sticks atop a wagon and watchin' 'em put the fire out, I ain't caused them no harm."

Henry said, "Walk toward that place where a wagon tongue's been run up beneath the wagon in front. Davis, you go on ahead, and call out when you're close or they'll shoot you." As Luther went past, he and Mullins exchanged a venomous look. Henry spoke to the captive again as Luther hurried onward.

"I'll hand you over to them and go back to find Amos."

"Don't do that, for chrissake."

Andy grinned in the darkness. "Maybe Amos and I'll get back in time to save you. Now stop talkin' and hold still."

Out where they halted, the darkness was deeper than it had been back where Mullins had been squatting in the grass to hurl his fire bundles. When they heard Luther Davis hail the wagons and heard a reply come back, Henry started the prisoner forward again with another rough shove.

By the time they got up there a crowd was waiting. Not a word was said as Mullins grunted over the wagon tongue.

Henry herded him past the silent, menacing settlers and halted him with his back to a wagon.

Luther Davis had already told about the fight and that Andrew Mullins was the renegade who had hurled the firebrands. Old Ben Fulbright cackled at the prisoner, "What you been eating, 'possum belly? Must be good living in them mountains. You know what's goin' to happen to you?"

Hugh Morton pushed up to confront the prisoner. He asked his name, then asked about the other raiders. No one missed Henry, not even Mullins, who had been pinning his hope of survival on him. By the time Mullins and Luther looked around for Henry, he was nowhere in sight.

The night was getting cold. Henry ignored this as he went about as far out as they had been before splitting up. He made a mournful night-bird call and waited. He had to repeat it three more times before there was an answer from another night-bird a long way to the west, over in the direction of the creek.

Henry hunkered down to wait. When a lumpy large silhouette appeared that he could skyline, he came up off the ground very slowly, wagging his head.

Amos was on horseback. He had not seen the last fire bundle nor heard the fight. He had scouted left and right, but mostly straight ahead in the direction of the creek, and had found the hobbled horse. When he swung off, he said, "Mullins is out here somewhere. This here is his outfit." Henry explained about Mullins as they started in the direction of the wagons, with Amos leading the horse.

They stopped twice—once, while Amos searched for his dwindling plug, the second time, when they heard a very distant shout that could have been made by Plume or one of his companions. It had sounded as though it came from the northeasterly foothills, or perhaps somewhere between the hills and the wagons. Whatever it signified was lost on the older men as they resumed their stroll, but not for long. It had come from within the compound.

There was no one at the wagon-tongue barricade. There was almost no sound at all as Amos coaxed his captured horse to jump over the tongue.

Henry stopped just inside the compound to gaze around. Loose animals were stirring dust; to their left, a woman's muted singing came from within a wagon, sounding as though she was crooning a lullaby to children. That was the only sound.

Amos tied the horse to a wagon wheel. Henry was standing wide-leggedly erect, like a carved rock, looking toward the distant southward end of the camp. There were people down there, mostly men with weapons to lean on, but there were also some women.

Amos came up, stopped chewing to stare, and quietly said, "God a'mighty!"

Following custom on the plains, where there were few trees or none at all, when wagon-camp tribunals held trials and pronounced a sentence of death, a wagon tongue was hoisted into the air in a slightly downward position and tied back on both sides with strong ropes or chains. The hangrope was run through the tongue's front loop, normally used for harness buckles, and the knot adjusted so that the condemned man had enough slack to sit on a horse, arms lashed behind his back. When the horse was smartly struck on the rump and jumped out from under him, the rope sang taut.

Amos spat, looked eastward in the direction of the fire ring and the barricade of barrels, and grunted in disgust as he said, "Not a damned sentry. How many men does it take to hang a man anyway? If Plume had a lick of sense he'd be swarmin' over them barrels right now. Henry?"

"What."

"Did you know they'd hang him?"

"No. Well, I wouldn't have bet my life on it, but I didn't think they would."

"Come along. Someone better get over to them barrels. Damn it, you'd think they'd never hung a man before."

"Most likely they never have."

Amos reached the far side of the compound, sank to one knee to peer over the barrels into the hushed darkness beyond, and wagged his head. "You knew Andy'd never come to a good end. So did I."

"Yeah. But what about his woman and their pups. What happens to them?"

"The same thing that's been happenin' to all the other widders and pups out here since we was young men. They get over it someday and find their place. Henry, Andy's woman won't be treated no worse without him than she was treated with him."

The crowd was moving clear of the hanging man. Amelia Henderson and Ben Fulbright walked slowly in the direction of her wagon. She was silent, but the old man wasn't. "Reminds me of one time in a place called Rockyford I seen 'em hang three fellers right in a row. Had to cobble together a special scaffold. Folks turned out for miles around. It was a big celebration. Womenfolk dressed in their Sunday best, chil'run with their faces shiny an' their hair slicked down. An' the preacher give a real stirrin' oration about the wages of sin and all."

"Ben! *Shut up!*"

He stopped in midstride, startled and big-eyed. Amelia Henderson stopped with him. She let out a rattling breath and in an altered tone of voice asked him to climb into the wagon first and call out to her when he'd draped a blanket over that poor dead man back near the tailgate.

People were moving, mostly tired or indifferent. The wagonmaster came over to where Henry and Amos were squatting, got down, and said, "See anything?"

Henry gazed around in disgust. It was darker than the inside of a boot out there. "No, nothing."

"But they're out there, Mister Potter. Mullins told us they was. Thirty-five of 'em armed to the gills and lookin' for scalps."

Amos leaned on a barrel. "Mister Morton, you done right by hangin' Andy Mullins. For lyin' like that if for nothing else. There aren't no thirty-five out there. There wasn't that many all-told up at the big meadow camp. And the last time I heard of hair bein' lifted was ten years back. Those men out yonder—exceptin' for maybe old Tenkiller—never even seen a scalping, let alone took part in one."

"How many then?" Morton asked.

"There was nine before you hanged Mullins," Henry answered him. "Now there's eight."

"Why don't they attack?"

Amos said, "Damned lucky for you they didn't, not havin' any guards back there while you was lynching Andy Mullins." Amos spat. "You better line out your armed men, Mister Morton."

CHAPTER 16
Darkness

Hugh Morton left Henry and Amos and walked over to where several men were peering in the direction of Coffee Creek and worrying aloud about thirty-five raiders out in the night. Amos did not hear the widow Henderson until she and Ben Fulbright were directly behind him. Her first words startled both the squaw men.

"What right had you to hit Mister Travis and leave him tied up?"

Amos turned, saw her hostile stance, and pushed up from behind his barrel. Henry did not arise, since Amelia Henderson was glaring at his partner. As he looked at them it came to his mind that whenever she walked up to him and Amos together, she never addressed him; she looked at, and spoke to, only Amos.

"You are a cruel and callous man, Mister Cardiff. He was groaning in pain when Ben found him and called me. His face was swollen where he told us you had beaten him. You left him there beside a dead man. He was terribly upset."

Henry came up slowly to his full height. "Did you turn him loose?" he asked.

Widow Henderson speared Henry with a hostile look before answering. "We took him out of the wagon."

Henry stared. "Which way did he go?"

Amelia Henderson's glare hardened toward Henry. "If you'll allow me to finish, Mister Potter! . . . We took him out of my wagon and chained him to the off-side rear wheel. He protested. I told him I'd find you two and get your side of it, and if it wasn't satisfactory I'd come back to turn him loose. Now then . . . Mister Cardiff . . . Why did you abuse him and leave him in my wagon tied like a shoat?"

Behind the angry widow, slightly to one side, old Ben Fulbright leaned on a rifle and seemed barely able to control his amusement. Amos ignored him. "Our side of it?" he said to Amelia Henderson. "Our side of it is that he's a no-good, sneakin', devious son of—"

"*Mister* Cardiff!"

Henry spoke. "He was meetin' that dead feller, who had a store in Bent's Siding, up at the big meadow. Sneakin' around in the night to do it."

"Is that against the law, Mister Potter?"

Both Henry and Amos were taken aback. "It's against our law," Henry finally said. "He'd found a vein of gold up yonder an' was storin' it up. That Butler feller snuck up in the dark for it, and gave Ned cash greenbacks."

Amelia Henderson turned back slowly toward Amos. "He found gold and was selling it. I'd guess two-thirds of the people out here would give five years off their lives to find gold, and as far as Ben and I know, selling raw gold isn't against the law."

Amos started to protest. "Amelia, he—"

"*Missus* Henderson, *Mister* Cardiff!"

"—Missus Henderson, he double-crossed his own people up there and—"

"What did you and Mister Potter do, Mister Cardiff? Oh, I am grateful for what you've done for us down here, but for all we know, Mister Travis didn't like the idea of a massacre any more than you two did. Ben . . . ."

Fulbright hoisted his rifle and started to turn away in the direction of the wagon. To Henry, it appeared that Amelia Henderson and old Fulbright had worked this out before approaching them. Henry raised his voice slightly. "Ben, don't you turn him loose."

A single gunshot sounded from the easterly darkness. A few people saw its flash, but Amos and Henry were facing in the opposite direction.

Old Ben Fulbright was lifted off his feet and dropped ten feet onward, his rifle clattering to the packed earth.

Amos whirled with a sizzling curse and led the widow to safety. He and Henry went to the nearest wagon, crawled beneath it, came out on the far side, and without a word passing between them moved apart as they began their manhunt.

In the compound, voices were raised, some in excitement, some in anguish.

Amos crawled fast. The grass was less trampled on this side of the wagons than it had been toward the creek. He made good time, but with the knowledge that the sniper who had painstakingly crawled close enough to see inside the compound was probably moving away even faster.

Also, because Amos knew the raiders, he did not for one moment believe the sniper was out here alone, as Andy Mullins had been.

Except for the agitated outcry back in the wagon camp there was not a sound as Amos continued his crawl. He knew they were ahead somewhere. He also knew they were on foot; if they'd had horses he would have abandoned his stalk. If they'd had horses he would have heard them departing, or at least changing their position.

He was gambling on their belief that settlers would not come hunting them in the darkness beyond their forted-up place. That Amos and Henry might do it had probably occurred to them, and if it had, they would be lying like lizards in the grass somewhere, ears to the ground.

He moved with care, in fits and starts, and he changed course often. Henry was somewhere southward. The odds were not pleasant to contemplate. Even if it was only the pair of full-bloods, Plume and Tenkiller, the odds were not particularly good.

Amos eased flat down, put his ear to the ground, and remained like that for a long while, until he thought he detected faint reverberations on his left in the direction of the uplands.

He remained perfectly still.

The outcry from the compound faded. Amelia Henderson had told Hugh Morton that Amos and Henry were gone, and he put armed men on the east side, scattered among the makeshift barricades and beneath the wagons, with orders not to shoot until they were certain anyone approaching from the east was not one of the squaw men.

Amos lifted his head inches off the ground, twisting it slowly from side to side. There was no movement. At least none that he could see. He was gathering both legs to move ahead at the same time he heard someone else doing the same thing on his left.

He drew his belt gun, eased flat down, and waited, but the other man was moving more easterly than southward and would not come close enough for Amos to see him.

The chill was seeping into Amos's bones, but he was barely aware of it. If he had been, it would have occurred to him that as the night wore along it got colder, which probably meant that it was late.

When he could no longer distinguish the sounds of the other man, he started ahead. If he could not hear, neither could the man he was stalking.

As he moved a yard at a time he speculated about which raider was ahead. He knew them all. What he was not sure about was whether Mullins had lied to Henry too, as he had lied to the settlers. If he had lied to Henry, and a couple of Plume's raiders had gone in search of the horses, then the field would be narrowed even more and the man he was stalking could be Plume himself. Or the old man. Either way, if Amos closed with him it was going to be a fierce fight. If it was one of the others, barring that gangling boy who had tried to kill him at the stone corral, it would still be a battle.

Like the man he was stalking as well as every other man out here, Amos had never had any crisis of conscience about killing. If he instead of the settler named Luther had found Andy Mullins, there would have been no lynching, because he would have killed Mullins on the spot.

Now, as he concentrated hard on detecting the faintest sounds up ahead, it seemed to Amos that his prey was not moving aimlessly. He did not alter course, nor did he halt. He seemed anxious to reach some particular point. If that were so, Amos could assume he was going to meet someone, which meant Amos had better catch him soon or turn away.

He rose up as much as he dared, peered through tall grass for movement, found it, and watched as the other man paused briefly, not to listen but to rearrange his gunbelt before starting onward again.

Amos eased up onto his haunches. He leathered his six-gun, drew his big knife, came up into a crouch, and covered two-thirds of the distance before he rolled two pebbles together underfoot and the other man halted to look back.

Thirty feet separated them as Amos sank hard down on both feet and catapulted forward, knife hand low and forward.

The other man did not jump up; he rolled frantically to the right, groping for his belt gun. Amos came down from above as the other man got his gun out and raised it to block the knife thrust. The fist and knife handle hit the gun hard enough to break the man's grip on it. It fell into the grass as the raider doubled his leg for a vicious kick.

Amos twisted slightly as he came down atop his adversary. The knee glanced off his hip. The man was wrenched partly onto his side. He reached desperately for his belt knife as Amos hauled back for a second thrust with his right hand while searching furiously for his enemy's knife wrist. He caught it, but his adversary was a strong individual and half dragged Amos as he put all his strength into raising the knife for a downward strike.

They were breathing in explosive grunts. The noise they made carried. Amos had to finish this quickly. He leaned high with his weight behind his knife, which was poised to slash downward, and strained to force the knife backward and downward.

Amos looked his opponent directly in the face. The man was Ruffy Barton. He was an unmarried 'breed who had been a friend of the Mexican.

Ruffy Barton did not make a sound or lose his look of murderous hostility even when he knew the knife was coming. They glared eye-to-eye as Amos felt his weapon slide off bone and pass through soft parts.

Ruffy Barton's legs flexed spontaneously; his entire body arched, went rigid for a moment, then sank flat out.

Amos sat back for a very brief moment before moving southward as swiftly and soundlessly as he could. He did not stop until his lungs were aching, by which time he was far enough from the dead man to feel safe, at least for the time being.

He sank belly-down, put his ear to the ground, and breathed deeply. Ten minutes later, with his heart pounding less, he started moving again, this time in the direction Henry had taken.

A wolf called in the dim distance, which made Amos stop moving. It had probably been a genuine wolf, but he waited for an answer nevertheless.

There was no answer, but something eastward rubbed abrasively over stone, just once. Amos shook his head before starting in pursuit again. He was hoping very hard it was Henry up there.

It was. They met as each man eased back on his haunches, looking into a gun barrel from a distance of about fifteen feet. Henry's breath eased out quietly as he holstered his gun and eyed his friend's rumpled appearance. He did not speak. Neither of them did. They got belly-down, side by side, and concentrated for a long while on just testing the night for sound or movement.

The cold worked on them. Henry nudged his friend and jerked his head. Amos understood and was willing to return to the compound, but leaned to whisper in Henry's ear. "They're eastward somewhere."

Henry did not reply, he simply jerked his head again and began moving back the way they had come.

Amos followed.

They had covered half the distance and could discern the old wagons, which looked disconcertingly like some variety of gaunt prehistoric animals in the watery starshine, when a wolf sounded, this time behind them somewhere but not as distant as the earlier call had been.

Amos increased his gait.

They stopped where the grass had been picked close by horses to look back and listen, but if anyone was trying to find them, they were not very close. Henry leaned over and whispered, "What the hell kind of a raiding party they got, the old man and his strongheart? Shoot once, then run away?"

Amos eyed his friend skeptically. "Don't make no mistakes. That old man never gave up on a raid in his life. If they're not doin' anythin' it's because they want it that way. It'll be a while before dawn. They got lots of time."

Henry started forward again, continued until he could make out details up ahead, and halted, this time to cup both hands and make a night-bird whistle.

Amos was leaning down when the gunshot sounded and a bullet cut ten inches above his back, where his throat would have been a moment earlier.

"You crazy sons of bitches!" Amos bawled in rage.

A man's deep voice rolled over the gunshot echoes as Hugh Morton yelled for no more shooting. The only person who did not heed the shouting was Amos Cardiff.

Henry grabbed Amos's arm and held him in place. "It was

an accident," he said, which he might as well have said in Greek for all the effect it had on Amos. Amos jerked his arm free and sprang to his feet.

Henry caught up with him at the barrels where Hugh Morton and several other men were standing. Amos slammed past the barrels and halted. "Who fired that shot?" he demanded of the settlers.

No one answered. No one ever did answer that question.

CHAPTER 17
Blood Is Black in Darkness

The settlers stood stoically, eyeing both squaw men. Henry, who was the most prescient of the two, asked Hugh Morton who had fired that shot. Morton's reply was succinct. "Fulbright died, shot clean through from back to front."

Neither Henry nor Amos was very surprised.

"And," continued the wagonmaster, "we talked to Mister Travis."

Amos spat and shook his head. "Mister Morton, I got to say this—you people aren't back east no more. You don't hold no councils when there's raiders sneakin' around your camp potshotting folks."

Morton was unperturbed. "Did you find anything out there?"

"There's more'n one," Amos stated dryly. "Only now the number is down to seven."

"You caught one?"

"Yes. A feller named Ruffy Barton."

The men looked owlishly at Amos but no one asked questions, which was just as well. But Morton had something else to say. "Mister Travis said you fellers beat him and robbed him."

Amos's temper was still high. Henry cut in before his friend could speak. "That there is a private matter. Between us and Ned Travis. It was like that before we got down here, and we'll take care of it."

Hugh Morton seemed to be considering this, when Amelia

127

Henderson came forward. No one heeded her until she said, "Mister Cardiff . . . He's gone."

Amos stared at her. "Ned? You set him free?"

"No, Mister Cardiff. His wife set him free."

Henry and Amos gazed steadily at Amelia until one of the men standing with the wagon boss said, "What in the hell has any of this to do with us, Mister Morton? What'n hell are we standin' around here for when there's renegades out yonder?"

Another settler muttered agreement. Amos and Henry pushed past and, with Amelia following, walked briskly in the direction of her wagon.

People looked at them, some even softly called congratulations on their safe return. They did not answer or slacken pace when Sun Sister appeared from the far side of the wagon, moving slowly. She saw them and ignored them, raising a hand to the side of the old wagon as she moved slowly along. Amelia Henderson went to her while Henry and Amos went out behind the wagon to the west to stop and listen.

Henry made the only comment. "That wasn't real clever of him. We still got his money, and if any of Plume's men come across him, he's goin' to look a lot worse than if you and me overhauled him."

A solitary gunshot sounded from the south, not very distant, and although it had been aimed at a man sitting carelessly on a barrel, when it tore wood from a wagon box eight inches from him, he dropped to the ground and did not react otherwise than to squawk loudly.

Amos led the way back to the compound. Ned would not stop now. The creek would shield him after daylight returned. As Amos watched Amelia take Sun Sister in both arms, Henry said, "Without a horse Ned's chances aren't somethin' I'd want to bet money on. If he's not just scairt, he'll wait an hour or so and try to steal a horse from here."

Amos shook his head. "He's not scairt and he's not crazy enough to try skulkin' back here for a horse."

Amos walked over to where the two women were standing, tapped Sun Sister lightly, and waited until she turned to face him. He said nothing. Neither did Henry. Amelia Henderson would have, but the longer she stood there watching the three people, the stronger became her conviction that what the squaw men and the lovely girl were doing had something to do with a private ritual. She moved over against the wagon and leaned there.

Sun Sister had been crying, but she was dry-eyed now as she faced the men. She was not defiant, but neither was she allowing anguish to show. In a quiet voice she said, "He wouldn't take me."

Henry inclined his head slightly, but remained silent. Amos shuffled over to the wagon to lean there. After a long interval during which the settlers at the far end of the compound helped the frightened man to his feet and got behind things as they tried to see or hear the renegade who had fired the shot, Amos addressed his niece. "I would have been surprised if he had, Sun Sister. A woman don't know a man as well as other men do."

"He said if I got the chains off him we could take two horses and get away from you and from Plume too."

Amos responded, "He might. He might get clear, Sun Sister. But you are better off than if he had taken you with him . . . Did you know he found gold in the high country, and that the dead man in Missus Henderson's wagon had been meetin' him out behind the cabin up yonder, givin' him money for the gold?"

She stared impassively and said nothing, but to the older men, who had known her since childhood, it was clear that she had not known.

Henry placed a hand lightly on the girl's arm. With surprising compassion he said, "I understand. I know. When your man does somethin' like this it just sort of destroys everythin' for you. I'm not goin' to tell you you'll get over it."

She looked at him, her eyes dull. "I can't believe he would do that. He—when I tried to hold him he knocked me down, told me we . . ."

Amos said, "Missus Henderson?" and the buxom widow came to take Sun Sister away. The older men watched them depart and would have talked, but three fire bundles came soaring. People yelled and Luther Davis tracked one with his rifle, fired, and blew the thing to pieces but did not put out its fire. Burning slivers went in all directions.

The people ran for water. One firebrand had landed in a fold of wagon canvas on the near side. Since Amos and Henry were closest, they beat the flames out with their hats and stamped on the pitch-splinters until they were out, while elsewhere others were doing pretty much the same thing.

But the objective had not been to start fires, it had been for the torchlike burning bundles to light up the inside of the compound, to provide targets for the men out in the night.

Gunfire came from the south, the east, and also from the west, in the direction of Coffee Creek. Morton roared for everyone to take cover. Amos added his voice by warning the settlers not to allow the burning pitch to background them.

The young woman who had befriended Sun Sister was running along the east side of the compound in the direction of the farthest wagon, when the gunfire began to increase, for although the defenders had nothing to aim at but muzzle flame, they were firing back.

She was passing a jumble of barrels north of the fire ring when someone on the east side, up close, caught her by firelight and fired. She went down.

Several women screamed. Sun Sister had seen the woman fall and ran to her across the open area without making a sound, caught her under the arms, and began dragging her toward the shelter of a wagon box.

The three men among the barrels were looking in the wrong direction, engrossed in what was happening inside the compound. They had not even fired back in the direction of the sniper who had shot the green-eyed woman.

Henry grabbed his partner's shirt to catch his attention, then ran rapidly across the compound with its flashes of brilliant flame and its turmoil in the shadowed places as people and animals rushed in all directions.

The sniper to the east, not far from the barrel barricade, had no reason to flee, since the defenders had not fired back. He stood up to his full height and aimed again. This time, though, one of the defenders glanced over his shoulder in time to see starlight reflect off a gun barrel, and shouted even as he struggled to twist for a shot.

He got off the shot, but not before the dark, shadowy man beyond the wagons had aimed and fired. Amos almost stopped when he saw Sun Sister stumble backward, away from the woman she had been dragging. Henry saw her fall, too, but he neither faltered nor heeded the defenders up ahead, who were now facing eastward, firing into the darkness. He bowled one man over and struck another so hard the man dropped his weapons and grabbed a barrel for support.

Amos came along moments later, as the startled settlers were recovering. He charged through them, too, but this time they got out of the way. When several women cried out for help with the two women on the ground, one defender went over to them, but the others remained at the barricade, trying to catch sight of the men who had raced so recklessly out of the compound. It was too dark to see far, but they could hear someone running.

The cold had been increasing for several hours. Each gunshot back among the wagons sounded particularly distinct, and up ahead of Henry Potter the cold air enhanced another sound: a fleeing man was not trying to be quiet, he was trying to outrun the sounds of pursuit behind him.

Amos, who was not built for racing, did his utmost but fell steadily farther behind. He could hear Henry, but could not see him.

The sniper, probably beginning to believe he could not outrun at least the man closest to him, stopped, whirled, and fired a Winchester.

He missed. Henry did not fire back; he put everything left in him to closing the distance. He almost made it before the sniper started running again, and now, finally, the man yelled.

Amos would have chanced a shot if Henry hadn't been in front of him in the darkness somewhere, but he ran now with a six-gun in his right fist.

Behind them the firing had developed into gun duels. Firing was less, and occasionally there were intervals when no one fired at all. Then someone would fire from beyond the wagons into the night, and someone else inside the compound who had been waiting for a muzzle blast fired back.

Henry was sucking air. The man up ahead was probably doing the same thing, but as he began to widen the distance between them a bitter thought occurred to Henry: he was chasing someone much younger than he was, and while age was of great benefit in some things, possibly in most things, it wasn't in a foot race.

He raised and cocked his six-gun, accepted the probable futility of what he was going to do, and fired anyway. The running man up ahead lengthened his stride. Henry was having a hard time maintaining his pace; he was not able to increase it.

But the bullet may have come close, because the fleeing sniper called out again, this time in words both his pursuers heard plainly.

"Shoot! There's two of them! *Shoot!*"

The only gunfire was back at the settler camp, and it was beginning to dwindle.

Henry ran with his mouth wide open and still could not get the air his lungs needed. He tried one more shot. Behind him Amos was beginning to lose ground. He had about reached his limit.

Up ahead, someone yelled and gun flame nearly blinded Henry. He had to slacken off because he could not see for several seconds. The muzzle blast had been close, perhaps no more than a hundred yards ahead.

He heard the sniper call out for the shooter to fire again, and dropped to the ground as the second blinding muzzle blast nearly deafened him. Far back, Amos roared like a bear and fired off three rounds in the direction of the muzzle flash.

When the echoes departed, Henry raised his head. He saw nothing and heard nothing. With surging hope he gathered himself to rise.

Amos was coming from farther back. He started to yell, but this time two Winchesters exploded almost simultaneously. Any outcry would have been indistinguishable against that kind of noise. Again, Henry was temporarily blinded, but he'd had a second to see a pair of dark silhouettes flat on the ground at the lip of a shallow arroyo.

Amos was no longer running. Henry's heart sank at what this could mean. Amos could die out here. They both could, but Henry was willing to if, before that happened, he could get two clean shots at the men on the lip of the arroyo.

He remained in place, waiting for the tumult inside his chest to lessen before starting to crawl. He was hoping as hard as he could that the snipers were not retreating. It was his anxiety about this possibility that finally drove him forward, right hand closed in a death grip around the saw-handle stock of his old six-gun.

The firing farther back was down to an occasional exchange. Henry crawled over rocks and spiny little shrubs, wondering which direction the attackers would take when they decided to give up and leave. There were too many guns inside the compound for them to win. When they stopped firing, he knew they were leaving.

A bull-bass roar from behind stopped Henry in a second. He ran a filthy cuff across his face, dropped his head to the ground for a moment in gratitude, then started crawling again.

The shout had been Amos. He had roared out a string of curses that would have made a teamster blanch with envy.

One of the snipers did a foolish thing; he fired in the direction of Amos's profane insults. Henry was caught again by blinding light, but he was also able to fix the location of the shooter in his mind. He pushed his right hand forward, waited for the blindness to pass, then emptied his six-gun in a ground sluice.

He couldn't hear a thing afterward as he rolled onto his side to pull out fresh cartridges, shuck out the casings, and replace them with fresh loads.

He still could not hear very well when Amos began cursing again at the top of his voice. But this time he sounded closer.

Henry pushed his gun arm forward and waited to cock it until he heard something along the lip of the little arroyo.

The only thing he heard was Amos coming. No one fired back from the edge of the little swale, and no one out there made a sound.

CHAPTER 18
A Cold Discovery

Amos hurled himself down beside Henry without taking his eyes off the place where he had seen those gun flashes. He was panting like a stud horse and, cold or not, sweat was dripping from his chin.

Henry wondered if the invisible snipers could hear his partner's breathing as well as he could, and finally said, "Crawl to the left. I'll go around the other way. If they don't hear us, maybe we can get behind them in that gully."

Amos put a restraining hand on his friend's arm. His head was up off the ground. "You sure they're still over there?"

Henry wasn't sure of much of anything at this moment. "No."

"I'll roll, try a shot, and roll again."

Henry did not have an opportunity to protest; as Amos usually did once he'd made a decision, he moved immediately to implement it.

Henry held his breath.

Amos fired at ground level from a distance of about fifty feet.

There was no answering fire. Henry could hear him grunting as he rolled.

Moments passed, Amos was stationary out there in the darkness, and when Henry expected him to fire again, he instead roared curses.

Still, no one shot at him.

Henry began to crab-crawl as fast as he could in the

direction of the swale. He reached it and slithered down its west bank, trying to guess how far he was from the place where the raiders had fired.

Amos was shouting again. "Who's over there, you woman-shootin' sons of bitches? I'm goin' to cut your throats!"

Every time Amos bawled, Henry scuttled. He got down into the arroyo and crawled northward, watching the upper bank on his left side until he was able to skyline a lumpy shape with its legs down the near side of the rim. He kept crawling until he saw another raider. This one was directly in front of him, lying on his stomach with his head up across one arm. He was staring directly at Henry from a distance of about twenty feet.

Henry's heart skipped. He dove flat and pushed out his gun fist. He had landed slightly to one side of the staring man up ahead, but the raider did not turn his head, he just continued to stare directly southward.

Henry cocked his weapon. The raider continued to stare southward. Henry pushed out a long breath and eased down the hammer. The man up ahead was dead.

Amos was turning the night blue again from the flat ground to the west as Henry crawled over, shook the raider, and pulled back as the man's head fell gently from his upflung arm to the ground. It was old Tenkiller. The bullet that had ended his life had hit him on a downward angle up close to the throat. He had died almost instantly.

Henry stepped over the old man as he started up the slope where the trouser legs were visible. He aimed and cocked his gun again from directly behind the other raider, and as before there was no response, not even a flinch. He grabbed an ankle and pulled the man down below the lip of land, just in case Amos heard him over here and fired. But there was no shot, just the sibilant whisper of a body being dragged over grass.

This one was also dead. He had been hit twice in the left

side. Probably when Henry's anger had made him ground-sluice until his six-gun was empty.

He remained below the lip as he straightened up and called to Amos. "They're dead. One is the old man. The other one is that young buck who come to the meadow from Montana last summer, the one they called Bighorn."

Amos walked to the rim and looked down, gun in hand. He holstered the weapon as he started down to stand with Henry to gaze at the younger raider, who had light coppery skin and braided hair. Amos spat and said, "Woman shooter!"

They went down where Tenkiller was lying, and squatted, gazing at the wide-open black eyes. Amos spoke as though the old man could hear. "You damned fool, I gave up on you long ago. There's something you could tell me, Tenkiller. You knew how many guns was down here, or pretty damn close, and you knew how many stronghearts would be with you'n Plume. You been making war all your life, so you had to suspect there was just too many of 'em down here. I don't care whether you looked at these people with contempt. You knew what happened to Colonel Custer for bein' contemptuous. Why did you do the exact same damned thing?"

Henry was sitting with his head cocked. Far back, the gunfire had ended. Since it was unlikely the settlers had defeated the other raiders, somewhere between Henry and Amos and the camp were more raiders.

Amos spat aside, leaned over to close the old man's eyes, then looked around. Henry nodded without speaking and led the way southward until the shallow place began to tilt upward and eventually became part of the level ground.

A bumbling east wind was blowing, cold enough to make the men flinch when it struck them. It was too dark to see very far; it was like being in the middle of a world of endless blackness. They knew the direction of the wagons and they also suspected that the raiders who had broken off the fight over there would be coming in this direction, probably under Plume.

Amos said softly, "How many left?"

Henry shook his head without answering.

At a very great distance, so great that it was barely audible, a horse whinnied. Both men faced around, but the sound was not repeated, so they did not know whether it had come from the east or from the timbered up-country that was more northward.

They did not discuss what it could signify. They spread out a little and continued south until it seemed they would be safely below the territory where returning raiders would be seeking their spokesman. Henry and Amos exchanged hand-signs as they turned westward.

It was a long walk. Neither man had any idea they'd gotten so far from the wagons. Amos, who was ahead, halted once and sank to one knee in the grass. Henry waited until his friend arose, wig-wagged, then resumed his hike.

The cold was particularly noticeable. So was the display of mocking stars whose dispassionate brilliance had never been sufficient to see well by, which had been both a curse and a blessing.

Finally they could make out the camp, barricaded with whatever had come handy, including treasured dressers and trunks, assorted wooden boxes and barrels.

Amos abandoned caution and angled until he and Henry were walking side by side. "Hour to daylight," he said. "If Plume ain't pulled out by now, he—"

Henry's hand closed like a vice around his friend's arm, demanding silence. He pulled Amos down with him and jutted his jaw.

A silhouette moved directly toward them, as though he might have come from the southerly area outside the compound. He moved soundlessly but with his head down, not up, not alert and moving.

Henry whispered, "If that's a settler . . ."

Amos grunted, made no reply, and got a little lower in the tall grass, concentrating on what he could make out in the blackness.

The little wind had shifted. It was now guttering along about belt-buckle high, coming more from the north than the east. Far back, a horse whinnied shrilly and the oncoming shadow halted, twisted to look back with his head up, his thick upper body easy to skyline, his right hand, which was holding a Winchester, loose at his side.

Amos sighed soundlessly and whispered, *"Plume!"*

Henry made no sound and did not move until the oncoming man resumed his hike. But now, instead of holding to a course that would have taken him down the front sights to the rear sights of the men hidden in tall grass, he changed course slightly, on a more direct course toward the arroyo where Tenkiller lay dead.

Amos whispered again, "He can't be the only one left."

As before, Henry did not make a sound. He was watching the strongheart, gauging distances. Plume had a Winchester. Henry and Amos had handguns. The distance a slug from a six-gun might travel did not have much to do with the distance a shot from such a gun was accurate, and Plume was moving away, not closer.

Finally, Henry whispered, "You go back, stay south of him. Don't make any noise until I've had time to get behind him, then catch his attention and hold it. Ready?"

As Amos turned back, Henry moved with extreme caution. He placed one foot gently down before moving the other foot. He had lost sight of Plume but knew his direction.

A long way northward a cougar screamed. Henry took several steps, then halted and sank down because he knew Plume would have also halted. At a distance it was difficult if not impossible to tell a genuine scream from a mimicked one.

Henry arose into a low crouch and moved again. This time

he had Plume in sight briefly because the Indian had been slower at striking out again after the cougar screamed.

To the right, ahead and southward, a faint sound of small stones coming together under a boot sole stopped the strongheart in his tracks. In an instant he was lost to sight, down in the grass. Henry stood motionless, waiting. When he heard the faintly grating sound again, onward and to his right, he took two long forward steps and palmed his handgun.

Plume appeared as a compact lump facing slightly to the right, holding his Winchester in both hands as he strained to locate the position of someone south of him who seemed to be walking in the direction of the wagon camp.

Henry could feel the jolts of his beating heart all the way to his feet as he raised the six-gun very slowly. The distance was acceptable, but the moment he cocked the gun the Indian would spring away with lightning speed. It was too dark for Henry to expect to be accurate against a moving target if the first shot missed.

Now Amos was no longer making any sounds. He too would be flat out in the grass somewhere; hopefully after he had crawled far enough from the position Plume was watching not to be hit if the strongheart tried a sound shot.

Henry's thumb pad was hard down over the gnarled dog of the hammer, when Plume eased soundlessly up into a low crouch and started in the direction of the sounds that had caught his attention.

His thick back was to Henry, head thrust forward, body tensed as he inched away.

Henry snugged his finger taut inside the trigger guard and cocked his weapon. Exactly as he expected, the Indian made no attempt to look back, and hurled his body sideways, hit the ground, and rolled frantically as Henry moved his muzzle and fired.

The noise was deafening. Distantly, Amos saw the flash and pressed close to the ground, waiting.

Plume's tumbling roll seemed to become abruptly less

controlled, more frantic. Henry hauled the hammer back without otherwise moving to track the thrashing figure. He was tightening his trigger finger again, when Plume rolled up to his feet, sidling to his right while he brought his Winchester around.

Henry was finally moving as he fired again, and knew he had missed even as he fired. Plume was swinging the Winchester to the left when he fired back. He had one moment to lever up the next load, when Henry, down on one knee, steadied up and fired his third shot.

Plume's body was wrenched violently half-around as Henry's bullet struck the chamber of his Winchester, ruining the weapon but saving the Indian from being shot through the lower body.

Henry yelled at him, "That's enough!"

Plume straightened up to his full height and hurled the Winchester with all his strength. Henry twisted swiftly to avoid being struck, and when he turned back, the Indian was raising his fist with a six-gun in it.

Henry fired twice as rapidly as he could pull the hammer back and let it slide from beneath his thumb with the trigger held fully back. The explosions were so close together they sounded like one continuous roll of gunfire.

Plume fell.

Henry cocked his weapon to finish the fight; the hammer fell on an empty casing. He jumped up, dropped the gun, drew his knife, and started toward Plume, who was struggling to sit up.

Amos walked out of the blackness behind the downed man and called to his friend, "That's enough. He's hit bad."

Henry halted, watching the strongheart in the grass. He sheathed his knife, looked back for his handgun, picked it up, and walked over to Amos, who was already on his haunches near the wounded man. Amos looked up at Henry, looked down at Plume, groped wordlessly through several pockets for his tobacco, and tore off a cud that he tongued into place while Henry leaned forward.

Plume had been hit twice. Evidently Henry's first shot had ripped along his ribs barely under the skin, while one of his later shots had struck the burly Indian closer in and higher up, through the lights.

Plume's fierce struggles weakened as Amos leaned, raised him by the hair, and propped him against a knee. "Take his damned knife, Henry," he said.

The strongheart was a man of powerful physique and unbending resolution. Had he been born thirty years earlier he would have counted plenty coup and made his name known from the Missouri River to Buttermilk Fort. His misfortune was the same as it was with many like him who had teethed on the stories of earlier times; he had reached manhood long after the period he cherished had ended.

He would die. All three of them knew that. But while Amos and Henry were willing to squat and wait, Plume was not. He called them every bad name he could think of in two languages. They squatted impassively, Amos propping him up and Henry loosely holding the knife.

When Plume paused for breath, Henry said, "Tenkiller is dead. Along with Bighorn. So is Andy. Now you."

"You two . . . I never trusted you. Travis too. I told the old man . . . you'd turn back, you'd go over to the whites."

Amos spat aside, continued to brace the dying man, and glanced over his head at Henry, who was now filling his little pipe. The infuriated strongheart started to scream curses, but the effort was too strenuous. Blood gushed from his mouth. He leaned dumbly forward, wagging his head like a gut-shot bear, and when Amos moved his knee, Plume fell slowly onto his side and died.

CHAPTER 19
First Light

They sat in the grass with the dead full-blood, oblivious of the little on-again off-again cold wind. Henry puffed up a head of smoke and Amos sat a moment, eyeing his depleted twist of molasses-cured before nibbling at it.

"How many are left?" Amos asked.

Henry acknowledged the question with a shake of his head, but this time he removed the pipe to speak.

"Depends if the settlers shot any."

"How many come down here?"

Henry wagged his head about this too. "Six, eight, maybe ten. Who knows? If there was more, the old man sure as hell sent someone to catch the horses, and with dawn light near and them wagons still standin' over yonder, whoever came through in one piece knows by now it didn't go right. They'll be headin' back to the meadow."

Amos tucked his neck deeper into the collar of his hide shirt, gazed at Plume, and said, "It ain't him so much as it was the old man. Plume, well, he was just too much of a strongheart, but the old man, the old damned fool, he *knew*, Henry. He didn't have to go over to that town. Everyone else who went there includin' you'n me, we told him. He heard other things. He had to know doin' somethin' like this would ruin everything, him included."

Henry puffed in silence. He had nothing to add. He straightened up to scan the east, but although it seemed there might be a faint paling in the sky, darkness still

143

prevailed. He turned in the opposite direction, toward Coffee Creek, removed his pipe to expectorate, plugged it back between strong, worn teeth, and gazed pensively at his partner. "Amos, if we don't come down with our death from runnin' around all night in the cold, it'll be a miracle."

Amos grunted.

"Tell you something else. This ain't the life for men past forty. Come morning you'll be too stiff to step over a scantling."

Amos's eyes came up. "And you won't be?"

"Yeah, I'll be. I can feel the cold seepin' into my bones right now . . . Amos?"

"I'm listening, and I got a hunch about what you're going to say."

"All right then. What's the answer?"

Amos sounded irritable when he replied. "I told you before, one of the other times you brought this up—I don't know. Except that I'm too old and set in my ways to learn farmin' and never liked the idea anyway. We're both too old to move into a town and learn trades. Henry, you know what Plume's trouble was?"

"Yeah. Like a lot of Indians, he let a white man creep up behind him."

"No, damn it. His trouble was that he wasn't livin' in a time he should have been born into."

Henry removed the pipe, peered into the bowl, leaned to knock out dottle, and was pocketing the pipe as he looked up. "You talkin' about us, Amos?"

"Nobody else is out here are they?"

Henry rubbed a grimy palm over salt-and-pepper beard stubble without answering. Finally, the bothersome little cold wind departed and Henry changed the subject. "Travis is most likely free by now. We should have searched him."

"We did. That money's hid under a wagon."

"Naw, his pockets. If Butler come out here to give him that money for gold Ned had already sold him, then Ned likely had another pouch or two for Butler to take back with him. He said that's how they done it. Ned would hand over the pouch, then go back to dig up more so's when Butler come along with the money Ned's got more gold for him."

Amos spat again and ran a filthy sleeve across his lower face. "Well," he said, as though making a pronouncement. "The son of a bitch's got a stake to start up with somewhere else."

Henry made a wolfish smile. "Amos?"

"What."

"You think that bastard'll keep on running? I don't. I wouldn't and neither would you, if we had a gold vein. He might stay away until this mess gets sorted out, but he'll come back as sure as we're sittin' here. He'll skulk back up yonder and maybe fill a bunch more pouches before he leaves the country for good. That's human nature, Amos, even for a sugar-cured son of a bitch."

Somewhere westward a sound like a man striking an anvil rode the still air. Moments later there was another sound, this time more like large pans of some kind being handled carelessly.

Amos shook his head and grunted up to his feet, gazing in the direction of the wagon camp. "No sense at all," he grumbled. "No wonder it was so easy for Indians to sneak up on settlers."

As they walked in the direction of the wagons Henry hefted the knife he had taken from Plume. It had poor balance. He reversed it, held the tip high, and hurled the thing northward. It clattered where it landed and Amos grinned. "I never knew anyone in my life outside of fire-ring braggarts who could do that—throw a damned knife and have it stick into a man."

Without the wind it was downright cold, and this fact was finally borne in upon the partners. They did what they could to mitigate cold—precious little, because their deerskin shirts were not lined.

Henry glanced over his shoulder. They were being backgrounded by watery, fish-belly light from the east. Dawn was coming, but it was not hurrying any.

Amos chewed and walked, swung his arms, and said nothing until they could see some details of the wagon camp ahead. All he said was "Hell, that noise was them folks digging. Probably burying old Ben Fulbright." He rolled his eyes. "Just like everything is over with."

Henry said, "It is. Whoever's left out here quit long ago if he had a lick of sense, and whatever else you can say, those broncos from the big meadow ain't idiots."

Amos scowled. "But the settlers don't know that, Henry. That's what I'm tryin' to say—they don't know it's over. Instead of keepin' watch for skulkers in the damned night like anyone with a pinch of sense would be doing, they're—"

The gunshot rang out, sounding more waspishly distinct than most gunshots when shooters used black powder.

Amos made a little gasping, choking sound and fell.

Henry was stunned, but instinct made him drop facedown in the grass even as he felt the first stirrings of fury. Someone up there at the wagon camp had fired that shot!

Henry raised his head and yelled, "You son of a bitch, it's us, Cardiff an' Potter! You hear me? It's Cardiff an' Potter! *Answer, gawddamn you!*"

There was a reply, but it was a long time coming. Henry strained hard to lift Amos, who was heavy anytime but was heavier now because he was inert. Henry could not cradle him and walk because Amos sagged through his arms, so he got him slung over one shoulder as a recognizable bull-bass voice called out.

"Come on in. Why didn't you yell? Let us know you was coming?"

Henry's stride was strong. The weariness he had increasingly been feeling since the little arroyo was gone. He was looking steadily in the direction of the barrel barricade as he marched along, Amos's blood soaking his shirt, Amos's hat back there in the grass somewhere, his arms and legs dangling.

Hugh Morton's next call was to the men around him to roll the barrels aside for Henry. Luther Davis was off to one side, leaning on his rifle with the bird's-eye stock, taking no part in the work.

The sky was shading from corpse-gray to a sickly blue-gray as Henry stalked past the barricade. Several women had come up, the widow Henderson among them. She raised both hands to her lips when she saw Amos, the blood, the slackness, but that lasted only a moment before she began to give orders. "You men take him. Careful, you clumsy oafs. Make a ladder under his back with your arms. There now. Follow me to my wagon."

With the load off his shoulders Henry felt light as a feather. There were five or six men standing close when one of them held out his hand with a bottle in it. Henry struck the hand aside, the bottle broke when it struck a steel wheel-rim, and the scent of whiskey rose up.

He looked from Hugh Morton, whose stolid features were beginning to crease into an expression of annoyance over the broken whiskey bottle, to the others, a man at a time. He stopped searching when he saw the gaunt man leaning on his rifle.

The sickly eastern sky was firming up with warmer and more noticeably pleasant colors, and it became increasingly easier to see out and around the countryside beyond the compound.

Henry did not make a sound as he lifted out his handgun to punch out spent casings and plug in a fresh load from his belt.

The settlers watched, as motionless as stones. Even the big wagonmaster was still and silent. When Henry was finished, he pointed the weapon directly at the gaunt man and said, "You ain't had time enough to reload it, have you?"

Luther met the older man's slatey stare the way a bird

returns the lidless stare of a snake. He did not speak at all, or move.

Behind them, out near the center of the compound, people were making a cooking fire inside the stone ring. Others were walking carefully among the wagons, peering beyond them when daylight finally made it possible to see fairly well.

Henry waited for Luther's answer, which did not come, so he cocked his weapon, and everyone within hearing distance of that unmistakable little snippet of sound froze.

"It ain't loaded, is it?" he repeated.

Morton spoke. "Mister Potter, put up the gun. It was an accident. It wasn't Luther's fault, it was your fault for not hailin' the camp. Anyone knows enough to do that."

Henry gave his reply without taking his eyes off Luther Davis. "Anyone knows enough never to shoot until they know damned well what they are shooting at. And that son of a bitch knows it best of all of you damned stump farmers, because to hit a man that hard he had to see him, had to see him real good—with the eastern sky gettin' pale behind him."

Morton had started to protest, when a gray, older woman, whose hair was straggling and whose weathered countenance showed the strain and fear she had recently been through, pushed in among the men to speak. She saw Henry Potter's cocked six-gun and slowly raised a hand to her chest, then forced herself to say, "Mister Potter, Miz Henderson wants you over to her wagon right away."

Henry looked away from the gaunt man for the first time since he'd addressed him. "What about? Can she resurrect a body, ma'am?"

"He ain't dead, Mister Potter. She wants you to help her. With Ben gone and all, she . . ."

Henry moved toward Luther Davis. He reached him before the big wagon master or the other men could intervene. Luther did not yield ground, but he was the color of putty as

Henry pushed the pistol barrel into his middle and with his free hand wrenched the handsome rifle away.

Hugh Morton snarled, and Henry turned swinging. The Kentucky rifle caught Hugh Morton in the side. He fell to his knees, making croaking sounds and holding his middle.

The other men did not move as Henry turned back and using Luther's gun as a prod, punched the gaunt man over to the stone ring, where a fierce fire was burning, halted him there as Henry eased down the hammer of his sidearm and holstered it, then raised the handsome rifle and flung it into the hottest part of the fire.

Luther could not salvage his rifle, so he turned on Henry with a roar of rage, and the squaw man was waiting. He turned his body in behind his right hand and fired it from shoulder height with his body twisting in behind the blow.

The sound was louder than the crackling noises of the fire as Luther's head snapped violently backward. His knees jackknifed, so that when he fell he landed on his knees for a space of seconds, head hanging forward. Then his body weight overbalanced him and he fell facedown in the manured dust of the trampled compound.

There was not a sound except for the fire. No one even looked up from the unconscious body of the gaunt man until Henry was striding in the direction of the widow Henderson's wagon, by which time the wagon boss had been helped to stand erect. With both hands clasping his injured lower parts he said, "Get hold of his ankles and pull him farther back from the fire!"

CHAPTER 20
The Day After

Inside, the wagon was crowded with boxes, sacks, and furniture. Sun Sister was with Amelia Henderson. They had stripped Amos to the waist and bathed him with heated water. When Henry climbed in, the women looked around without speaking.

Although daylight had brightened the world outside, there was no direct light in the old wagon with its ash bows and canvas cover, although visibility was adequate. Henry leaned behind Sun Sister. The rifle bullet had hit Amos on the left side. All Henry had been able to see earlier was blood, enough of it to convince him his friend had been mortally wounded, but with better light and the work the women had done on Amos, it was plain that the bullet had struck him on the left side, traveling on a curve. It had followed the contour of his body beneath the skin and his ribs. It was a nasty-looking, badly swollen, and discolored injury, but the women had stopped the bleeding. What made it look particularly bad was that Amos's bathed skin was ten degrees whiter where it had been covered by his shirt, than his face, hands, and neck.

Sun Sister arose and with averted eyes pushed around Henry to leave the wagon. Amelia Henderson ignored Henry to watch the girl briefly, then she also pushed past toward the front of the wagon.

Henry squatted. Amos's face was too naturally ruddy to show paleness, but his eyes were closed, he appeared unaware of what was happening around him, and his chest rode and fell in shallow sweeps.

Henry leaned closer to study the wound. While he was doing this Amos said, "One of them steel-jacketed bullets. If it'd been one of them lead ones it would have blown me in two."

Henry slowly turned his head. When their eyes met, he shook his head. "Them women got long faces. They most likely think you're dying."

Amos acted tired. "Yeah. Well, I thought I was too until Miz Henderson poured some of old Fulbright's whiskey down me . . . I didn't want to spoil things for them so I just lay quiet with my eyes closed."

"Does it hurt?"

"Not bad, no. A little when I take a deep breath, so I take a lot of little short ones. How does it look?"

"Like somebody caught you around the side with a shot-crimped bullwhip."

"Who done it?"

"Luther Davis, that scrawny bastard." Henry finally eased back. Amos did not move his head, but he followed Henry's movement with his eyes as he said, "They're going to boil up some beef broth for me. They set the whiskey jug above my head somewhere. You see it?"

"Yeah. It's back there against a crate. You want some?"

"Pour some into the tin cup they had with it."

Henry obeyed, then tipped the cup very slowly so Amos could drink without raising his head. When the cup was empty Henry put it back beside the jug and got comfortable eyeing his friend. "You're lucky. I thought sure you was about dead when I picked you up."

Amos rolled his eyes to see his partner's face. "Weak is all. And sore. What's goin' on outside?"

"They're loadin' up their wagons. Some of the women-folk . . . How come Sun Sister was in here? She got shot last night. Her and that lady who's taken a liking to her."

"Naw. Sun Sister didn't get shot. She was walkin' backward, draggin' the other lady, and fell over a singletree some darned fool left out there. Yeah. For a fact it sure looked like it, didn't it? She went down right when the bronco fired. But the other lady, she got hit up alongside the head. She only come around a short while ago. Her and their scout, that feller we set free up yonder, Dave Law. Sun Sister's nursin' both of 'em. They're in the wagon that belongs to the green-eyed lady and her man."

Henry reached inside his shirt to scratch vigorously. "You sure picked up a lot of gossip in a short while. Bein' shot an' all."

"I just lay here like I was dyin' and listened to their talk while they was washin' me and tendin' the wound. Henry, the widder Henderson's got a touch as light as a feather. Real soft. She's real fine at nursing, too."

Henry eyed the jug, leaned for it, swallowed twice, and put it back. He wiped his lips while gazing at his friend and said, "You lost a lot of blood."

Amos nodded. "Yeah. Sun Sister's goin' to wash my shirt. Lots of blood. Makes a man feel puny. Henry, hand me the jug . . . No, on the right side."

Henry watched his old friend tip the jug with one hand, drink from it, and put it down. Amos smiled. His color was better, but it had never been very bad. "Put it back, Henry. If she comes back I wouldn't want her to think I'm a drinkin' man."

Henry obediently placed the jug where it had been before, then blew out a long breath before saying, "Amos, you want to know what I think?"

"Every time you say that I know I'm goin' to be told what you think, so I don't answer. All right, what d'you think?"

"That you're a damned old fraud."

Amos's eyes widened. "Fraud? Look right there. You see the size of the swellin' and the bad color an' all?"

"Amos, when I come in here you was lyin' there, barely

breathin', with your eyes closed . . . Just now you lifted that jug of whiskey one-handed and set it down the same way. You're not weak. Well, not real weak anyway. You're play-actin'."

Amos licked his lips, settled his head comfortably on the rolled blanket the widow Henderson had placed beneath his head, and smiled. "They're makin' a lot of noise out there, Henry."

They were, for a fact. Henry climbed back down and saw that people were breaking camp. Sun Sister was helping to load. When she saw Henry she came over, looked up at him, and said, "They want me to go with them."

He looked around. No one was heeding them. Near the fire ring the wagon master was talking to four men armed with picks and shovels. Henry looked down at her. "Do you want to go with them, Sun Sister?"

"I don't know. I—don't know where I belong."

Someone whistled. The reaction was similar to the reaction of squirrels when a soaring hawk inspires the squirrel who sees it to squeak the alarm; people stopped and turned in the direction the lookout was pointing. Henry and Sun Sister turned, and Henry grunted.

A rider astride a big, stud-necked, pudding-footed draft animal was riding toward the camp from the southwest. Brilliant morning sunlight made it possible for the silent, motionless watchers to make out details. Henry squinted for a moment, then addressed Sun Sister. "I meant to tell you to find the widow Henderson so's the pair of you can tend Amos. He looked real peaked when I left him a few minutes ago."

Sun Sister turned away at once and ignored the approaching rider to find Amelia Henderson. When she found her, both women hurried to the Henderson wagon.

Henry moved to a place where a wagon tongue had been lowered, walked out a few yards until the approaching horseman saw him, then raised an arm to beckon.

Behind him Hugh Morton said, "You know him, Mister Potter?" and before Henry could reply, Morton added a little more. "That's the feller who staked a claim around the foothills easterly. Looks like he's got a pack behind his saddle."

Henry nodded gently while murmuring to himself, "Yeah. The axe man." Louder, and without looking around, he responded to Morton's remark. "You saw him heading away a few days back, didn't you?"

"Yes. We didn't ride out and palaver an' he waved but didn't offer to turn aside."

"You know his name, Mister Morton?"

"Gus Muller."

Henry nodded.

Morton came out beyond the wagons to stand near Henry as the twelve-hundred-pound horse plodded up and halted when his rider eased back slightly on the reins. Muller looked from Henry to Morton, did not say a word nor nod; he twisted, jerked free some ropes holding the ungainly canvas bundle, and gave it a rough shove.

The bundle landed hard. Muller leaned on his saddlehorn, gazing at the wagon master and the squaw man, still silent. He shook his head and had started to rein around, when Henry moved quickly, caught both reins behind the curb strap, and halted the big horse. He looked up at the bleak man in the saddle as he said, "There's a hand stickin' out of that wrapping, mister . . . Who was he?"

Muller's reply was curt. "See for yourself. Let me tell you something. You might want to pass it on to your partner too. There ain't a livin' man who can waylay my wife when she's kneelin' at a creek and try rippin' off her clothes and come out of it alive. Let go of them reins."

Henry did not relinquish the reins, but he slackened his grip as he gazed at the dead man, whom the wagonmaster had unwrapped. It was Ned Travis. He had been shot through the brisket. Death must have been instantaneous.

Henry removed his hand from the reins as he looked up again. "Tell me somethin', Mister Muller. Did that feller visit your camp a time or two when you was over on your claim?"

"Yes, he did. And I seen him back in timber shadows a time or two when he didn't come out, just sort of sat in there, watching."

Henry nodded because the answer confirmed his suspicions. Ned had been fascinated by the redheaded woman. The settler scowled menacingly. "Any more questions, Mister Potter?"

"Did you go through his pockets?"

"No. I tossed his gun aside. Otherwise, all I wanted to do was haul him up here and let you folks have him. We got no time to bury him and don't like the idea anyway. I know he came from here by his tracks . . . First, I thought he was tryin' to steal a horse, him bein' on foot, and maybe he would have if he hadn't seen my wife alone at the creek, drawin' a bucket of water . . . She screamed and I shot him."

The coldly angry settler turned back the way he had come without nodding or looking back. Hugh Morton draped the canvas back over the bloodless face of Ned Travis. "I got a burial party organized to go out yonder and bury the other ones. They can do the same for this one . . . You knew him real well, didn't you?"

Henry was kneeling when he replied, "Yeah. Mister Morton, don't bury any of them. We'll load 'em on horses and take 'em back to the big meadow. Bury them up there. You can lend a hand loading them."

Morton turned as someone called, then started away. Henry groped in the dead man's pockets but found no pouch of gold. He stood up with the noise of people striking camp reaching him, considered the dead man dispassionately, and started back.

The settlers worked swiftly, their uppermost desire to leave this place as quickly as possible. Amelia Henderson sought Henry to tell him agitatedly that Amos would not go with the settlers and she did not want to leave him here, in his condition, to be hauled up into the mountains on a horse when he would surely start bleeding again.

Henry spoke of something different. "That bundle out there in dirty old canvas is Sun Sister's man. He's dead. The man who brought him here shot him. I'd take it real kindly if you'd go stay with Sun Sister for a while. I'll go talk to Amos."

Amelia Henderson turned to watch Henry stride in the direction of her wagon, then reluctantly approached the wagon of the green-eyed woman, where Sun Sister had been staying.

The loading was becoming noisy, so perhaps the fear was finally being replaced by something else. There was even a little laughter, but not among the burial party when their wagonmaster told them to locate the corpses, bring them to the camp, and lay them out side by side.

Henry sank wearily down inside the wagon. Amos looked steadily at him for a moment, then spoke. "Now what?"

"Ned's dead. That settler with the redheaded wife shot him along some creek southwest of here. Backtracked him and left him lyin' out yonder covered with canvas."

"Why'd he shoot him?"

"For tryin' to grab his woman . . . And he didn't have no pouches of gold on him."

Amos stared without blinking. "That's what the settler said?"

"Yes."

"Don't mean a damned thing and you know it."

Henry was philosophical. He'd never seen the gold, and it hadn't been his. "All right. He lied. As far as I'm concerned he can have it. Before he gets where he's goin' he'll need it . . . Amos, the widow-woman says—"

"Henry! I can hear 'em hitchin' up. Go out there and climb under where I cached that money. It's shoved under the binder block in back. Get it before they start drivin' and someone sets his binders an' grinds that money to dust. *Go get it!*"

Henry did not move. His expression was calmly impassive. He ignored Amos's sudden agitation. "Widder Henderson don't want to leave you lyin' back here in the grass when they leave. She said you refused to ride with 'em."

Amos's eyes bulged. "Go get that money, you consarned old—"

"Why won't you go with her, Amos? With old Ben gone, she'll need a man to help with the outfit and all. An' you're sweet on her. And she can nurse you."

Amos's exasperated expression changed subtly. "You got any idea where Oregon Territory is?"

"A little, I guess."

"That's where they've decided to head for. Henry, everythin' I ever heard from the old trappers and hunters is that it never stops rainin' in Oregon. An' for chrissake, it's southwest of here until a man can't go no farther without drownin'. I told her to just set me out on the ground, I'll be fine."

"She's not goin' to believe that, Amos. Not after you looked so poorly and all, and got her to believin' you are dying."

"I'm not goin' to Oregon! I'm not goin' nowhere but right here!"

Henry rose. "Amos, Miz Henderson is fond of you. By the time you two got out to—"

"Henry! You want to go to Oregon Territory?"

"No. Never did want to. I'm goin' to take the dead back to the meadow for burial."

"You think I ought to go out there and learn the farmin' business?"

". . . No, I don't. But that's your decision. I'd sure miss you, what with your complainin' all the time and—"

"I'll bring the widder up to the meadow with me," Amos announced.

Henry shook his head. "You lost too much blood. Your brain ain't workin' right. You can't get this wagon up there.

There is no way, and unless she's addled too, she wouldn't abandon it down here and traipse to the big meadow with you."

Amos heard someone talking a team back onto a wagon tongue and almost sat up, forgetting his wound. When the pain arrived he sank back but rolled his eyes. "Go get that damned money. It's goin' to get ground to dust if you don't."

Henry finally went forward to climb out of the wagon.

CHAPTER 21
Hitch Up!

The man who owned the wagon adjoining the Henderson rig was Luther Davis. As Henry sauntered up on the off-side of his outfit, Luther did not see him, but when he crawled beneath the wagon someone else saw him and called to Luther, pointing.

Henry found the cache, stuffed Ned's money inside his shirt, and was crawling out when he met two booted feet. He looked up, saw Luther's bleak expression, and crawled around his feet.

Luther demanded, "What was you doin' under there, loosenin' bolts?"

Henry considered the tall, gaunt man for a moment in thought. After today they would probably never see each other again. He was more philosophical now than he had been when he'd hurled the handsome rifle into the fire, an act that he regretted, although he had no regrets about flattening Luther.

He said, "I left somethin' under there before me'n Amos went scouting last night." As he watched Luther's expression change slightly, he added more. "I've seen them back-east rifles before, but I never owned one. Where I been most of my life, they don't often show up for sale."

Luther's mouth drooped in bitter recollection. "Good reason. They cost more'n men out here got."

Henry inclined his head slightly. "I expect you're right. How much would a rifle like that fetch?"

159

"Seventy-five dollars."

Henry blinked. A lot of pothunters and trappers did not make seventy-five dollars in half a year. He fished inside his shirt, snagged some greenbacks, counted out one hundred dollars' worth, and held them out.

Luther Davis looked stunned and made no move to accept the money until Henry said, "Take it." Luther took it. Neither of them spoke to the other again, ever.

Henry was still standing by Luther's wagon when Hugh Morton came up, neither friendly nor hostile, just impassively stolid. "We found them dead Indians. They're laid out on the outside of the wagon to the far side of the stone ring. I got a couple of men waitin' to help you tie them on your animals . . . Mister Potter, it hasn't been an easy relationship, but the folks are beholden to you'n your friend."

Henry nodded a little woodenly. He and Amos had done everything that had been required. Morton and his settlers had done a lot less. Most of what they had done had amounted to heightening the confusion.

"We took up a little collection, Mister Potter, and we'll make sure Mister Cardiff gets good care on the trail out to the northwest." Morton held out a little buckskin pouch.

Henry gazed from it to the big man's face. "Amos won't go with you. He told me that no more'n half an hour back." He pushed aside the hand holding the little pouch. "Keep it. You're a hell of a long way from bein' out of the woods yet."

He walked down to the wagon where Sun Sister was sitting in shade, alone and impervious to the noise and activity.

He sat down beside her. She did not acknowledge his presence, and for a long while he simply sat there. Eventually he took her hand in his; it was like holding a dead bird.

"I'm going back to the big meadow, Sun Sister, to take Tenkiller, Plume, and the others to be buried."

"They will kill you," she said softly.

"Maybe. I don't think so . . . There's going to be a lot of wailing. Did Miz Henderson tell you about Ned?"

"Yes."

"I'll take him back up there, too."

"I'll go with you."

"You don't want to go with the settlers?"

"No. I don't belong with them. I'm not sure where I belong, but I was born and raised here. This is my place, Henry . . . What about Amos?"

Henry heard men shouting on the wagon's far side and ignored it as he replied. "Well, Miz Henderson wants him to go with 'em to Oregon Territory. He told me he won't do that."

"She is very fond of Amos. Did you know that?"

"Well, yes. I didn't come down in the last rain. A man notices things. But if he won't go with her, I doubt that she'd stay behind when the others pull out."

For the first time Sun Sister turned toward Henry. "She will stay with him. She is very worried about you moving him. She will stay behind and care for him."

"Did she tell you that?"

"Only that she worries about him. But I am a woman, Henry. I know a woman's heart, red skin or white skin."

The noise in the compound was louder. Henry sighed and shoved up to his feet. Smiling downward, he brushed the handsome woman's shoulder and went back into the sunlight.

On the east side where the barricades had been removed there were horsemen, eight or ten of them, rough-looking men armed to the gills, still wrapped in thick riding coats against the earlier cold.

Henry recognized one of them. He did not really know the man, but he had spied on him several times, watching him erect his fortresslike log house on Coffee Creek. His name was Charley Knight. He was a raffish man, unshorn and beard-stubbled. As Henry crossed toward the stone ring, Knight and his companions eyed him. Hugh Morton told them who Henry was and what he had done, he and his wounded partner.

Henry did not offer his hand; he nodded at Knight, ranged a look at the hard-eyed men clustered around, and asked a point-blank question. "You been a while gettin' here. Have trouble, did you?"

Knight's eyes slid away from Henry as he replied gruffly, "Had to get my horse shod. He was tender like he was walkin' on eggs by the time I got to the town. An' it took a spell to get these gents rounded up to ride back with me . . . You're one of the squaw men from up yonder, ain't you?"

Henry barely nodded. "Squaw man" was not a term used casually or flatteringly; Knight knew it as did everyone else. "I'm from up yonder," he replied, and looked from man to man among the townsmen. They looked straight back, unbending and stonily quiet. "Somewhere around here there is a feller named Fred Butler. You gents from the Siding most likely know him. He's dead. You may want to take him back with you."

A bull-built, graying man with very dark eyes raised his brows. "Butler? What was he doin' out here? He's got a shop in—"

"There's another dead man," Henry said, interrupting the black-eyed man. "Him and Butler was close friends. He'd know why Butler rode out here, but like I said, he's dead, too."

A younger townsman jerked his thumb as he asked who the dead men were lined up outside the compound. Henry explained that they had been part of the raiding party and that he intended to take them up into the mountains to be decently buried. Then he walked away, leaving the townsmen watching him with interest and suspicion.

Hugh Morton opened up to them a little more about what Henry and Amos had accomplished. It appeared to satisfy even Charley Knight, but there were still questions. Morton answered them as best he could. Some of them he could not explain away because he did not know the answers, and right now, with most of the wagons loaded and ready, he had more important things to do than answer questions.

Charley Knight remained with the riders from Bent's Siding, uncomfortable about having brought the townsmen this far to rescue people who clearly did not need rescuing. He offered to return to town with them and stand all the drinks. It was not an offer that appealed strongly to men who had ridden a considerable distance to fight, had sustained themselves on that long ride with growly boasts, and now were practically ignored by the people they had come to save. On the other hand they were rough, hard-living men; disappointment was part of their everyday existence. They were also hard-drinking men, so Knight's offer, which was better than nothing, was agreeable to them. One or two of them turned their horses to mount as they accepted, which left Charley Knight, who wanted to stay home, with no alternative that was not awkward, so after a quick glance back, he swung up with the others and headed southwest toward the distant settlement.

Some of the settlers watched them ride away, past the dead chestnut horse on a ranging wide curve around the eastward slopes. Henry watched until Morton strolled over, settled comfortably against a wheel, and spoke while watching their would-be rescuers growing small in pleasant sunlight. "We buried that other one. The feller we hanged. If we'd known you figured to take them into the mountains for burial . . ."

Henry fished for his pipe, got it fired up, and savored the raw bite of Kinnikinnick before speaking. "Don't matter, Mister Morton. He wasn't a feller a man'd care to dig a very deep grave for."

"The others were, Mister Potter?"

Henry removed his pipe to look into the bowl. "Somethin' I learned long ago, Mister Morton, is that sometimes the man best able to make a decent judgment is the feller who's been on both sides. They had their reasons. We had ours,

Amos an' me, and you had yours . . . I'd say those bodies I'll bury up yonder belonged to men who figured they had a right."

A gangling man with a shock of unruly auburn hair came up, nodded to Henry, and spoke to the wagon boss. "Everyone's ready to roll except the widder Henderson. Couple of us offered to harness her horses and make the hitch." The young man's eyes flitted to Henry before he continued. "She said she'd stay here and look after Mister Cardiff. She told us he's bad off an' shouldn't be moved. She said we owed him that much."

Hugh Morton looked blankly from the shockle-headed man to Henry, then on down the line to the only wagon that did not have animals hitched and ready to move.

Henry felt the big man's quandary and knocked his pipe empty as he said, "I'll go talk to her, Mister Morton. It hadn't ought to take long."

Morton nodded his approval and started toward the opposite side of the compound. The sun was climbing fast now; there was warmth and almost limitless visibility. It was the kind of day wagoneers prayed for because the customary obstacles they encountered—swollen watercourses; rough, deep, miles-long arroyos; mud—either did not appear or could be avoided. The settlers were ready to roll, impatient to be on their way, to get clear of Coffee Creek, to head away from forested slopes and gloomy uplands.

Word passed among them why Hugh Morton had not given the order to move out, and for a while they were patient, but the longer the delay, the less patient they became.

Henry sat with Amelia Henderson on the high seat of her wagon half in shade, half in sunshine, oblivious to the restlessness around them as he spoke slowly, marshaling every objection he could think of to dissuade her from remaining behind when the others departed.

She listened politely, did not interrupt, and kept facing

forward so that Henry addressed her iron-set profile. As he was finishing, Sun Sister came along, climbed in, and made her way toward the tailgate, where Amos was lying with his head cocked to pick up every word being said out front.

Sun Sister sat down. When Amos met her gaze she quietly said, "They have the bodies tied across the horses on the east side. I don't think Henry should take them back to the camp, Amos. There will be anger. They will want to kill him—and you."

Amos smiled thinly. "You never tried to talk an idea out of Henry's head, did you. It can't be done."

"I'll go with him."

"So will I. As soon as these settlers get on their way and—"

"No, you won't," the handsome young woman said quietly but resolutely. "You will stay here. You can't ride that far. You would start bleeding again."

Amos looked hard at the shadowy face. "Lie out here in the damned grass?"

"No. Widow Henderson will care for you."

Amos's eyes widened. "Did she say that? What happens when everyone heads out an' she's left behind?"

Sun Sister ignored the questions. "She is a fine woman."

"I know that, but stayin' back, alone and all—"

"She is fond of you, Amos."

For a long moment the older man said nothing. He could hear the solemn conversation continuing out front, but made no attempt to listen.

Sun Sister reached, passed him a crockery jug, waited until he'd downed a couple of swallows, then took it back, stoppered it, and placed it aside. She smiled so softly Amos could barely make it out in the interior of the old wagon. She also placed a cool hand on his arm as she said, "I am not old enough to be wise, like Tenkiller's woman, but I have learned something here. If someone really cares for you . . . doesn't just use you . . . if you let them get away you will regret it."

She removed the hand and lost her faint smile.

Amos could feel her pain as though it were his own. He fumbled for her hand and squeezed it. "We'll look after you. When we go back up yonder, we'll look after you, Sun Sister."

She freed her hand, and turned abruptly to work her way forward, ignoring Henry and Amelia Henderson as she eased around them and climbed to the ground, her eyes wet-bright. She moved quickly outside the trampled place, so no one could see the slow-coursing tears.

Several men stood in a small group inside the compound, talking solemnly with Hugh Morton and Luther Davis. The morning was wearing along. They did not know where they would find water before evening, but after they left Coffee Creek it could possibly be many miles and none of them wanted a dry camp. They did not want to wait any longer. The widow Henderson's decision, they told Morton, should not be allowed to delay and possibly even endanger the others.

The man who spoke bluntly to them was not Morton, it was Luther Davis. "One day ain't goin' to make any difference, even if we had to waste all of it, and we won't. But if we did have to waste it, you gents had ought to be thankin' whatever you believe in for them two squaw men, because without them, my guess is that most of you would have been killed last night."

Luther walked away, leaving an uncomfortable silence in his wake.

CHAPTER 22
The Parting

Henry stuffed his pipe, fired it, and saw the look on Amelia Henderson's face as the blue smoke drifted past. He continued to puff. Amelia Henderson was not the first individual he had encountered whose wrinkled brow and averted nose signaled aversion to his pipe. Even up at the camp only a few women were not annoyed when he fired up. Fawn Tenkiller was one.

Amelia said, "I appreciate your loyalty to Mister Cardiff, and your advice to me, I appreciate that too. Mister Potter, have you ever abandoned an injured person?"

He was watching the shockle-headed man who was married to Sun Sister's green-eyed friend. The man was talking to Morton and waving his arms. "No ma'am, I never have. But Amos won't get abandoned. I'll take him back up to our village in the big meadow."

"I've told you that kind of a trip could cause him to bleed to death. But even if the wound didn't open up, he's a very sick man. You can see for yourself how puny and all he is."

Henry puffed furiously before removing the pipe to look into its bowl. If he said Amos was a fraud, wasn't really as bad off as he'd let her believe he was, she'd maybe snatch him bald-headed. He returned the pipe to his mouth and bit down on it so hard that when he replied the words sounded unnaturally short. "Well then, Miz Henderson, the others'll roll and you'll stay here with your wagon alone, and you already know this ain't a country full of friendly folks. And with Amos so sick an' all, he couldn't protect you."

"I can protect myself, Mister Potter. Do you know how far I've come doin' just about everything but shoeing my own horses?"

"No ma'am, but—"

"No buts."

Hugh Morton appeared beside the front wheel, looking up with a frown. "Amelia?"

"I will stay back, Hugh. Maybe I'll catch up later, but for a spell, at least until Mister Cardiff is able to make it again on his own, I'll stay back to look after him."

Morton glanced past. Henry removed his pipe, raised his shoulders, let them drop, and replugged the pipe between his teeth.

The wagon master shifted stance, clearly reluctant to have the matter end this way. He was about to speak when Henry said, "I'll come back an' look after her, Mister Morton. Once I get shed of my other chores, I'll come back down here."

Morton's expression indicated that he was not entirely satisfied. Two men called to him, the shockle-headed fellow and a burly, bearded man who was braced on the seat of his wagon, lines in hand, booted right foot on the binder-handle, ready to kick the brakes loose. Everyone was packed, loaded, hitched up, and impatient to depart.

Morton looked upward, wearing a worried expression. For the last time he addressed the widow Henderson. "You can follow our tracks, Amelia, or you can ask along the way. We'll leave word . . . May God look after you. Good-bye."

Henry watched Morton raise and lower his arm. The wagons moved ponderously; there were several shouts at animals that were slow responding to a gee or a haw. Children walked with some of the people, mostly women, and sunlight added to the picture. Then Henry's attention was caught by a slight sound, and he turned. The widow Henderson was holding a balled-up handkerchief to her face. He knocked his pipe empty, pocketed it, and arose to climb back inside the wagon. There was nothing he could say to someone sitting in the middle of nowhere, watching people she had lived alongside for maybe half a year or longer move with heart-wrenching slowness out of her life forever.

Someone had freed the pucker-string on the canvas above the tailgate. For a change there was sunlight inside the wagon. Amos was staring straight up when Henry pushed around and squatted. Amos said, "Look out yonder."

Henry craned beyond the tailgate and caught his breath. Sun Sister was back several yards, sitting beside a bedroll on the ground where a wagon had been.

Amos spoke. "Law. They set him out when they was ready to roll. Sun Sister's mindin' him like Miz Henderson's minding me."

Henry returned to the small place and squatted beside his friend's pallet. "They left him behind because they don't figure they'll need a scout from here on?"

Amos's moving eyes came to rest on his friend's face, showing bleak amusement. "No. They left him behind because he told 'em to. He didn't want to go to Oregon Territory, either."

Henry studied his friend's expression until understanding arrived. "He wants to go up yonder with us?"

Amos's expression hinted at exasperation. "While you been fussin' around with them settlers, I been lyin' in here listenin' and puttin' things together. Dave Law wants to go wherever Sun Sister goes."

Henry raised his hat to scratch as he said, "Oh . . . well . . ."

"Henry?"

"What?"

"You get rigged out. We can't leave Plume and the others tied over them horses with the sun beatin' down on 'em. You get rigged out and as soon as I can get dressed we'll head up into the timber."

A quiet voice sounding as though it was made of pure iron

spoke from the front of the wagon. "Amos, your britches and whatnot are locked in the possible-box on the outside of the wagon. You're not going anywhere until you're healed."

Amelia Henderson worked her way back and stood above the pallet, ignoring Henry and staring fixedly at the wounded man. Amos looked up, then skittered his gaze elsewhere. He cleared his throat. "He dare not go up there by himself, Amelia, specially bringin' back the stronghearts who was killed down here. They'll—"

"Then he'd better stay here, Amos. Him and Sun Sister. But that's up to him. You're not going. Not with that—look under the bandage—that wound's puffed up like a flour sack. It's purple halfway up your carcass both ways, but it's closing and there's no infection, thank God . . . Amos, I didn't let those folks go so's you could ride off and bleed to death somewhere in the mountains. You are going to stay right here!"

Henry pushed upright. He might as well have been invisible for all this movement meant to the widow and Amos Cardiff.

She suddenly knelt down beside the pallet and spoke in a softer tone of voice. "I haven't asked anything of you, Amos, and most likely I never will—just don't kill yourself."

Henry did not have to see her face, or even hear her words. Her tone of voice reached his heart. He turned without another word to his old partner, climbed out of the wagon, tipped his hat against dazzling sunlight, and saw Sun Sister walking toward him. Beyond her the lump in trampled grass where David Law lay on his blankets was limned on each side by wide steel wheel marks.

He walked to meet her. She jutted her jaw in the direction of drooping horses standing hip-shot and dozing, all but three burdened with shrouded dead men. The three that were not wore saddles. All the animals had been hobbled.

Henry frowned in that direction. When Sun Sister came

up, he said, "Keep them other two horses here. All I need is my own."

Sun Sister's reply was direct. "David and I will go with you."

Henry's scowl went to her face. "You told me up yonder he'd lost a lot of blood. Sun Sister, I'm goin' to have my hands full, leadin' those horses. If I got to look out for a man who's too weak to be riding . . . Naw, you an' him stay here with Miz Henderson an' Amos."

"He told me if Amos can't go with you, then he'll go."

Henry flapped his arms. Henry could see David Law's head turned in his direction. "You tell him he's goin' to stay here if I got to hogtie him. For chrissake, it was easier fightin' off Plume an' the others than it was tryin' to talk sense into anyone down here."

"Then I will go with you," the beautiful woman said, her face showing gentle resolve. "You will need help with the horses. Amelia can look after Dave and Amos."

Henry felt like swearing. By this time he should have been a mile or two up into the mountains. "An' suppose," he told her dryly, "someone comes along. She's got some right valuable harness horses. And she's a fine-lookin' woman. And she'll have two wounded men to protect her."

"I am going with you."

He stood looking at her. He had known her since childhood. She was quiet and gentle. She had humor and strength. She was wise for being young. He had long felt that she deserved someone better than she had got.

He made one last effort. "They're goin' to be killin' mad up there."

"If you didn't think there was a chance, you wouldn't go, Henry."

He squinted at the sun. The day was still young, but it was a long ride to the big meadow, longer going uphill all the way with burdened horses. He could not possibly reach the camp in daylight.

Sun Sister said, "I'll go take off the hobbles," and walked away.

Henry walked down to the wagon, but did not reach for the wheel hub to climb up. He looked over the tailgate. Amelia was feeding Amos. She had propped him up. Neither of them was speaking, so Henry said, "Mind now. Keep watch. Bring the horses in at night an' tie 'em real good. Amos . . ."

"You be mighty careful, Henry. They are most likely already wailin' and whatnot up there."

Henry walked across the trampled place that had been the compound, took a set of reins from Sun Sister, waited until she was astride, then handed her the lead-shanks until he had mounted.

They struck out toward the timbered uplands with hot sunlight coming downward at the morning angle. Both of them looked back a time or two, until they could no longer do that because leading packed animals into a virgin forest allowed no time for anything except what was immediately required.

Buzzards were circling, still very high, above the carcass of the handsome chestnut horse Butler had ridden. Otherwise the sky was empty and so was the land.

When they had been climbing for about half an hour, Henry reined over into a little level glade with tall grass and halted to "blow" the horses. He handed his reins to Sun Sister, walked southward until he could see far out and around, then watched some very distant ant-sized wagons waddling southeasterly, dwarfed to insignificance by the hugeness and emptiness of the land.

Much closer stood the Henderson wagon. He remembered the axe man because he could see Amelia chopping wood in the meager shade of the rig.

He shook his head, made his way back to where the horses were cropping grass, and stood beside Sun Sister as he said,

"I'll tell you what I figure. I figure that the raiders who got back to the camp with news of what happened down there started things moving. There was talk before we left that if things went bad the people would make a run for Canada."

She gazed up at him. "I was told that. Fawn said her man was out of his head to talk like that."

Henry took back his reins, snugged up some cinches, and led off out of the tiny glade back into the timber. It was hard going; because the huge trees were so close together, Henry had to sashay constantly to find places wide enough for the laden horses to pass through without bumping their loads.

But it was much cooler in the timber than it had been back down where the Henderson wagon was. And it was fragrant and nearly without sound. Occasionally a bushy-tailed squirrel appeared high above to scold noisily what he considered to be trespassers in his particular area. Other times, as they passed across lightning-strike clearings, hosts of nesting birds rose up, making enough racket to let every critter within a half mile know they were coming.

Henry's head dropped to his chest several times. Farther back, Sun Sister called to him each time this happened. She eventually called a halt, dug some jerky from a saddlebag, and told him to chew it, which he did. He did not doze off after this, but he had been a long time without sleep. By the time the little sunlight that penetrated the cathedral-like gloominess came on a late-day slant, Henry could have gone to sleep standing up.

What kept his mind alert now was the distance remaining to be traversed. They had been unable to make exceptional time, but because they had limited their stops and pushed steadily along, by Henry's estimate they would reach the final tier of big trees on the west side of the big meadow about midnight. He told Sun Sister that when they got up there he would leave her with the horses and scout up the camp.

She had nodded without speaking. It was becoming increasingly difficult to pick their way through the huge trees, because what little light there had been up until now had begun to diminish, foreshortening their vision. Sun Sister concentrated on passing along, not on anything else. Not at this time anyway.

CHAPTER 23
Toward a New Day

An hour before they reached the final tier of big trees they detected the diminishing aroma of smoke from cooking fires.

By the time they halted, it was cold as well as dark. Henry passed his reins to Sun Sister and scouted ahead. Across the big meadow there were only two pinpricks of light, and as he stood with his back to a shaggy fir tree, one of those lights died. The remaining one was southward. He watched it for a long while. It came from either Tenkiller's cabin or one of the houses close to it.

He turned back to explain to Sun Sister his plan of slipping into the village on foot. When she heard this, she said, "There are dogs, Henry."

He nodded. There were always the dogs; they barked at nocturnal raccoons, skunks, badgers, and airborne scents. He could not recall a night when they hadn't barked.

"Henry, why not go over there from the lower end, put down the bodies, and leave?"

His reply to this was not satisfactory, but Sun Sister had to be content with it because he turned to tying the animals, then scuffed up a bed of needles, sank down upon it, tipped his hat over his face and spoke from beneath the hat. "Wake me in a couple of hours."

She went among the animals, loosening cinches a little. The horses were hungry and thirsty. They had been tanked up and allowed to pick grass heads on the way, but there hadn't been a lot of pickings and less drinking water.

She moved soundlessly to the last rank of trees, sniffed at the fading wood-smoke scent, and watched the one remaining light across where the log houses stood. She was still there an hour later when a dog barked, the sound softened by distance. True to dog-nature, other dogs also started to bark. There was not a breath of air stirring, so the dogs had not picked up the scent of the laden horses or their two-legged companions. She watched a scimitar-moon, and when it seemed sufficient time had passed she went back to kneel beside Henry's nest and gently shake him.

He lifted the old hat, gazed at her through semidarkness, rolled over, and pushed a trifle stiffly to his feet. He looked across the meadow. The solitary light still glowed. "Somebody's mourning," he told the woman. She offered a simple reply. "Tenkiller's woman."

She accompanied him southward among the trees until he halted where he intended to move out into the treeless meadow. She touched him. The dogs were still intermittently barking, but that was not on her mind. "Be careful, because not everyone over there will be sleeping soundly."

He patted her shoulder and started walking.

In the distance a horse whinnied; it set the dogs off again. What would really set them off would be the scream of a mountain lion, but nothing like that occurred as Henry strode directly toward the solitary light. He used it as his sighting point. He did not actually require it to locate the camp. He'd returned many times in darkness over the years, but that light was like a lodestone.

It was a long hike, but he walked briskly so the cold would not bother him. Also, his nap had helped. He was not at all drowsy by the time he could make out the distinct dark blocks that were the log houses. By this time he knew where that light was burning. At Tenkiller's house. His woman would be awake.

But Henry veered northward along the rear of the other

houses to see how many corrals back there had animals in them.

Not very many. In fact most of the empty corrals had gates sagging open.

He stopped at the lower end of the settlement, and gazed at the light. His estimate was that about two-thirds of the people had abandoned the village, heading for Canada probably, but whatever their destination, gone in a hurry after receiving word of the fight down near Coffee Creek.

This was what he had wanted to ascertain before crossing the big meadow on horseback. In fact, this was what had encouraged him to come up here with the dead raiders. If the full-bloods had fled along with anyone else who had reason to fear the arrival of the army or a lawman-led posse from Bent's Siding, then those who remained would pose much less of a threat to him.

He hitched at his shellbelt, reset his hat, and crossed through pale starlight to the west side of the village, heading directly for Tenkiller's house. The light seeping around the slab door did not seem very bright when he was close to it. Less bright in fact than it had seemed a mile away. He went completely around the house before halting finally in front of the door. The scent of wood smoke was strong as he moved up and raised a fist to knock.

There was a long delay before he heard someone on the inside raising the *tranca*. When the door swung inward, the light made him squint, but he was clearly visible to Fawn looking out at him. She moved aside for him to enter, without either of them saying a word.

She closed and barred the door, passed him on her way to the cooking area, and as he sank down at the old table she brought him a cup of hot coffee, which he cupped in both hands for the warmth. Henry looked steadily at her across the table. She had her hair loose, and with the old lamp behind her she looked twenty years younger.

She looked straight back, expressionless and waiting.

"I brought him back. Him, Plume, and the others who were killed down yonder. They're on horses over yonder in the trees."

"Alone?"

"No. Sun Sister is with me."

"Her man?"

"He's dead."

"Amos?"

"Wounded. He's still down there bein' looked after by a settler widder who stayed back when the others pulled out. A fine woman, Fawn. She's taken a fondness to Amos."

"And you, Henry?"

"Tired clean through . . . When did you hear what happened down there?"

"This afternoon. People went running in all directions. Someone said there was a big posse of armed men coming. People loaded horses and went north. It went on right up until evening. Is there a posse coming?"

"No. Not that I know of. Some men came out from Bent's Siding, but went back. It was all over by the time they got down there. How many are left in the village?"

She did not answer until she had gone to the cooking area for another cup of coffee, which she brought back to the table with her. She sat looking at him for a moment before speaking. "I don't know how many, but only a few. The ones who were willing to face armed possemen."

"Mostly 'breeds?"

"And whites. No full-bloods. What will happen now, Henry?"

He sipped coffee before replying. "I don't know. I'll help with the burials. Maybe if those settlers find a military post they'll tell their story, so maybe soldiers will come. And maybe not. I don't know. Most likely one of these days some riders will come nosin' around up in here from Bent's Siding. Do you want to leave, too?"

She lowered her head to the cup in her hands. "No . . . will you leave now?"

He drained the cup and pushed it away. "No. I was never a fugitive. Amos and I could have left anytime the last five or ten years. This is our place, Fawn. Whoever might come up here, we'll meet and talk to them. We weren't among the raiders, we were against them from the beginning." He waited for her to lift her head, to meet his gaze, and when she didn't, he said, "I think Amos will come up, when he's healed enough for the trip. Maybe the widder woman will come with him. I don't know."

Fawn's handsome head finally came up, black eyes stone-steady in their regard of Henry. Something that had been strictly held back between them for many years showed faintly in her gaze. "You never ate right. And you are filthy now and your eyes have bags under them." She jutted her jaw. "Go lie down. I'll find Sun Sister and bring in the horses with her."

He had been succumbing to the pleasant warmth of the room for half an hour, and the drowsiness he had held off by napping was returning. The coffee that should have helped him remain alert had not functioned that way at all.

"I'll go," he told her. "You might not find her in the darkness."

The black eyes showed derision. "I could find her if I was blindfolded. You are worn out, Henry."

"A little tired," he conceded. "Who's left who'd want to shoot me for takin' the settlers' side down there?"

"No one. Even the full-bloods didn't blame you or Amos, they blamed my man and Plume. Mostly Plume." She arose. "Bar the door after me, blow out the lamp, and lie down. I'll let you know when we get back." She was braiding her hair with both hands over one shoulder as she stood looking down at him. "You take a bath tomorrow and I'll wash your clothes."

He stood up, reddening. "That bad?"

"Worse," she replied, fumbling among some attire hanging from wall pegs for a horsehide coat with red wool lining. She was shrugging into the coat as she went to the door. From there she said, "Blow out the lamp first."

He obeyed, heard her take down the *tranca*, open the door, and move away. He wanted to say something, but when he groped his way to the opening she was no longer in sight.

He closed the door, went to the pallet in the corner, kicked out of his boots, tossed aside his hat, draped his weapon and shellbelt from the back of a chair, and dropped down atop the bed.

He had no recollection later of going to sleep, and when dawn cold crept in around the door and the cabin's two tiny windows, he burrowed deeper among the blankets and hides, but sleep was beginning to elude him. He had a nagging feeling in the back of his mind.

He remained among the warm coverings for a while, watching a cold, gray false dawn arrive with its opaque light, then shoved upright and sat at the table to pull on his boots and buckle the shellbelt and holstered six-gun into place. He built a little kindling fire on the hearth, placed the coffeepot beside it, and rummaged for food.

He was not a good cook. Neither was Amos, but they had gotten by. He did not make much of a meal now, even though he was very hungry, and he ate it from a tin plate held high in one hand as he left the cabin and walked around behind it, scanning for the women and the laden horses.

The village burial ground stood north and slightly west of the meadow, in a stand of big trees. It had about a dozen graves marked by wooden headboards.

By the time Henry arrived someone had built a fire to offset the chill. There were three or four men up there, a few children, and some women. Sun Sister and Fawn Tenkiller stood slightly aside with them. The laden horses had been stripped and taken somewhere to be corralled and fed.

Men dug in solid silence, women stood away from the

blanket-shrouded corpses, and children either stared in big-eyed wonder at the cocoonlike shrouds of the dead or would not look at them at all and clung to their mothers. The time for wailing was past.

When Henry arrived, people knew he was there without looking directly at him. There was no greeting. The diggers continued at their work until one man, somewhat crippled with swollen joints and gnarled hands, climbed out of a hole and handed Henry his shovel.

Henry climbed down in and dug with the other men. There still was not a word said.

CHAPTER 24
Ten Days

Henry returned from bathing at the sump hole used for bathing and laundering, feeling better but still worn out. Tenkiller's woman had a hot meal waiting. Before she allowed him to sit down to it she handed him a rider's coat of horsehide lined with wool and told him to take off his clothes and put the coat on.

He obeyed, sat down to eat, and watched her roll his clothing into a ball and leave the cabin with it. They had said very little since returning from the burial ground.

Sun Sister appeared as Henry was out back sluicing off his dishes. She stopped dead still, looking at him. Between his boot tops and the bottom of the coat about six or eight inches of spindly shanks were exposed. He hadn't shaved, either, and his clean hair thrust in all directions. She let nothing show on her face, but it was a struggle.

She wanted to go back down to Coffee Creek. He could think of no objection, nor did she require his permission, but they went around front, entered the cabin, and sat down as he said, "Suppose he don't want to come up here, to stay up here? They're a different breed, Sun Sister. By nature they're restless. Amos and I was scouts too, long before you was born."

"If he has to keep moving, I'll move with him, Henry," she said, then paused to look at the hands in her lap. "He's not like Ned."

Henry rubbed the tip of his nose. Most likely she was right.

In fact, in Henry's view a person could rummage through a big pile of sons of bitches and maybe still not find another one like Ned Travis. Henry gave a little start that made Sun Sister's eyes widen. "The damned money's in my huntin' shirt. The inside pocket!" he exclaimed.

She started. "What money?"

"Three thousand dollars in greenbacks Ned had around his belly in a belt. Sure as hell Fawn'll scrub the shirt without lookin' in the pocket."

He sprang to his feet. She looked up at him. "If she's at the hole I'd better go. If you run outside looking like that . . ." She stood up and turned toward the door. Henry was still standing there for all the world like a clumsy big bird wearing someone else's old coat. She smiled at him. "I'll hurry. I'll bring the money back here to you."

He sank back down at the table. She could reach the sump hole before he could anyway. Henry went searching for a bottle of whiskey. He did not find one. He knew old Tenkiller kept one around. What he did not know was that after her man had taken down his weapons and gone out back to saddle a warhorse, refusing to listen to his woman's pleadings because he was fortified with whiskey, Fawn had taken the jug out among the trees and smashed it.

He had to settle for black coffee.

His intention had been to sleep while Fawn was down at the creek; he still had not caught up on his sleep. But right now he was too agitated. After two cups of bitter black java he went to the doorway and leaned there until he saw Sun Sister returning.

She smiled as he moved back so she could approach the old table. She put the soiled greenbacks in front of him as he eased down opposite her, and said, "She turned your shirt inside out before soaping it. All she said when I walked up and asked about the money was that nobody could have that much money and be honest."

"Did you tell her Ned had it?"

"Yes."

"What did she say?"

"Nothing. She was kneeling over a big rock. But her face showed that she still believed an honest person could not have that much money."

Henry looked at the greenbacks. "It's yours. He was your man. You inherit from him."

Sun Sister sat like stone, regarding the crumpled bills. When she spoke again it had nothing to do with the money. "I should start back now, otherwise I won't get out of the trees before it's too dark to see."

Henry put his hat over the greenbacks on the table and went with her to Tenkiller's corral, where she selected a horse. He helped her rig out the animal and watched her mount it. She looked down at him. "I think he will stay, Henry. He told me about his life. He is an orphan. He told me he was with those settlers because he wanted to be with people. He said someday he would build a house and maybe hunt a little, and have a family."

Henry nodded at her. "Be careful. When he's able to travel—him and Amos—if you send word to me I'll meet you somewhere down the trail."

As he watched her ride through brilliant sunlight across the big meadow, Fawn came up beside him without a sound and also watched. He shook his head. "She told me in the cabin she wanted to be with that scout, Dave Law."

"That's where she is going now?"

"Yes. Back down to Coffee Creek to stay until him and Amos is fit to ride up here . . . Fawn, when we was settin' in your house I told her scouts are shiftless, restless men."

She looked up at him. "Only the young ones, Henry."

He frowned at her. "That's not what I'm tryin' to tell you. There I sat, warnin' her, and she never said a damned word until we come around here to rig a horse for her. Then she told me he wants to have a cabin and settle down with a family."

"What's wrong with that?"

"Nothing. There I sat warnin' her and talkin' like an idiot because I didn't know her man."

Fawn brushed his arm as she turned back toward the house. "When I was a child and the pox left me an orphan, an old woman took me in. Her name was Firefly. She told me many things. Once she said that every day of our lives we are fools at least once . . . Come along. Your clothes won't be dry until this afternoon. You sleep now."

He followed her, but after she had entered he lingered a moment just beyond the doorway, looking northward, up where diminishing spindrifts of smoke from breakfast fires still arose into the still, golden brilliance. Farther away to the north were the eternal uplands with their crevasses of soiled ice, their cold shade and canyon shadows.

The irregularly spaced log houses in their emerald setting, the few people moving, dogs and children busy in new-day warmth in the nearer foreground made a picture that had never failed to make Henry feel completely at one with this insular world.

Ned Travis's gold vein was up there somewhere, probably hidden because Ned had been a sly individual. But men as old as Henry and Amos had learned long ago how to interpret every leaf, every brushed-out trail, every ruse two-legged and four-legged creatures used to conceal things.

They could find Ned's gold vein. Maybe not this year, but next year or the year after.

Fawn spoke from the shadowy interior of the house. She had picked up his hat. "This is more money than anyone in the camp ever had at one time."

He walked in, glanced at the tabletop, raised his eyes to her face, and told her in detail where the money had come from, how Travis had acquired it, and concluded by saying that by all rights the money belonged to Sun Sister.

She sat down, ignoring the greenbacks. "Gold up here?"

He gestured. "Somewhere northward."

"White people go crazy for gold, Henry."

He knew that. "Only if they know where it is."

"You aren't going to look for it?"

He smiled into her eyes. "Why should I? . . . I'm sorry about Tenkiller."

She raised his old hat in both hands and turned it slowly. "He was a brave man, a good hunter. When we were very young he was a good warrior, too." She continued twisting the old hat without looking up from it. "You tried to tell him. I heard you. I knew he was not going to listen. He was already planning to make a raid."

"Did you talk to him about it?"

She stopped twisting the old hat and replaced it over the greenbacks before meeting his gaze. "I am older than Sun Sister. She can talk straight out to her man. I couldn't. He wouldn't have allowed it if I had tried. I said a little, but not very much. But Tenkiller knew how I felt." She straightened back a little. "Go lie down and sleep."

He slowly arose from the table, smiling wryly at her. "You couldn't tell him to do that."

"No. But he was Tenkiller and you are Henry." She met his gaze.

It was ten days before a man feeding horses in late afternoon saw riders coming out of the timber a mile eastward and sent a child to warn Henry, who was shaving behind his cabin at the creek.

By the time he got out front there were several people standing as motionless and silent as statues, watching the riders. It was impossible to make out details because the sun was down, which veiled the big meadow in shadow.

He went over to stand with Fawn. Henry fired up his little pipe. Fawn spoke to him without taking her eyes off the oncoming riders. "They come slowly."

Henry removed his pipe to remark about that. "Two of 'em aren't in no condition to go faster."

She looked at him. Over the years Tenkiller had told her several times that Henry had eyes like an eagle. "How many?" she asked.

Henry did not look down at her. "Four."

"No. I can count six or seven horses."

"Four people, Fawn. Six horses." His little pipe had lost its fire, so he held it in his fist. "Amos, Sun Sister, the scout, and the widder-woman I told you about. An' two big draft horses carrying packs."

She lingered a short while before mingling with the other watchers. The riders, she said, would be hungry and tired.

There was some movement but not very much until one rider loped ahead. The watchers finally recognized Sun Sister. The women went with Fawn to make a big supper, and the men shuffled closer to Henry, still with nothing to say until he mentioned the need of the oncoming horses for feed and care.

Sun Sister appeared from between two cabins, reined in the direction of the men, halted, and smiled at Henry from her horse's back. "We left in the dark," she said. "We would have got up here sooner, but Amelia made us stop often while she looked at Amos's wound."

Henry nodded, saying dryly, "And it was all right."

She dismounted. A dark hand reached for the reins as she turned to watch the others coming through deepening dusk. Henry fired up his cold pipe again. There was a smell of burning wood coming from the communal fire ring.

When David Law rode up, Sun Sister reached for his reins and got close so he could lean on her as he dismounted. Amelia Henderson brought up the rear with Amos. Henry eyed his old partner skeptically, and when two men moved in to help Amos down, Henry removed his pipe, spat, then plugged the pipe back between his teeth. Amos had good color. If he'd lost weight Henry could not discern it.

Amelia Henderson looked around, first at the double row of log houses, then at the big meadow she had just crossed, and finally at the men who were leading their animals away. Not until Amos addressed Henry did she look at him.

Amos wagged his head. "Where is everybody, Henry?"

"Where you see lights and smoke, that's all there is. About half or better left when word come up here about what happened down yonder. A family or two come back over the last few days. No full-bloods come back yet."

Amos accepted this information. "You run into trouble, did you?"

"Nope. There hasn't been a whole lot said to me since I returned, but what has been said blamed Plume and the old man for puttin' everyone in danger."

Amelia Henderson broke in with a slight scowl. "Mister Potter, Amos needs to lie down. That was a hard ride for a man in his condition."

Henry's gaze slid from the buxom widow to his old friend. They exchanged a long stare; Amos's facial expression showed nothing, but his eyes twinkled ironically. He took Amelia's hand and started over toward his cabin. Henry heard him say, "Wait'll you see it by daylight. Prettiest place you ever saw. You'll like the people too."

She did not reply, but continued to clutch his hand.

Henry was left alone. He knocked his pipe empty, considered Tenkiller's house, but turned toward his own cabin because there was no light in the other residence and no smoke rising from the mud-wattle chimney.

With considerable care he lifted out a short length of slabwood in the corner near his stove and retrieved a whiskey bottle. He brought it out very carefully, replaced the slab covering of his hidey-hole, and placed the bottle on a shelf. He then took kindling from a bucket and got a fire lit in the stove. With that done he took the bottle to his table, sat down, and worried the stopper out with his teeth.

Dusk had passed, nightfall was down, and Henry's single candle did not cast much light but it was enough. He sipped whiskey and gazed out through the open door. He did not think of the gold vein, the money over at Tenkiller's house, the men he had helped bury; he thought of loneliness, of things from the past, of somber things until a fulsome silhouette appeared in the doorway and said, "What are you doing?"

"Sittin' here."

She entered, but stopped several feet from the table. "Everyone is at the fire. There is plenty of food."

He nodded without speaking, so she came closer, stopped across the table from him, eyed the bottle, eyed his face, and spoke again. "It is over, Henry. It is finished, but the camp is still here. So far no soldiers have come. No posse riders. Maybe they never will."

He said, "They will, Fawn. Someday they will. Something like that gets talked about."

"That's what you are doing tonight? Sitting here with your heart on the ground?"

"Well, not about that so much. Do you like the widder woman?"

"Yes. Everyone likes her. She is ruining Amos."

Henry chuckled. "Yeah, for a damned fact. Well, Amos hasn't been a young man in over half a century, Fawn. Seems to me a man's got a right to get spoiled in his time of sundown."

"Come back to the fire with me, Henry. They miss you out there."

He did not move. "What about Sun Sister?"

"She has a man. I think a better one than before. He told me he wanted to stay up here, to live up here with her."

As Fawn finished speaking, she put her head slightly to one side as she gazed at Henry. "The whiskey made you unhappy. What have you been thinking of—riding out, Henry? Leaving?"

He hadn't thought about that at all, but he did not answer as he sat there relaxed, slouching on the table as he gazed at her. "The dead men left women, maybe children."

She nodded. "You know how that's always been. For longer than anyone remembers warriors rode away and never returned. The others helped raise their children and looked after their widows . . . Henry, what is it? The whiskey?"

"Naw, couple of swallows has been my limit for years. You ought to know that. You never saw me drunk."

"What then?"

"Sit down, Fawn."

She remained where she was, watching him and waiting.

"It's been a long time."

"What has?"

"Well . . . lookin' at each other. Never saying anything, but looking."

Her answer was less brisk than her other words had been up to now. "You know why. While your woman was alive I didn't want to be looking at you. After she died it was a little different but not much. Now . . ."

"Yes?"

"Look at me, Henry."

He did and softly smiled in the feeble light. He guessed what was coming and spoke to head it off. "I've looked at you for many years and you haven't changed, except that now you are alone too."

Her eyes did not leave his face. "Someone will come looking for us."

That was probable. He arose from the table, took the bottle to his flour barrel and shoved it downward, beat flour off his arm and turned back. Her eyes had not left him. He smiled at her. "You sure did a fine job washin' my shirt an' all. It's as soft as when it was first made."

"Do you want to go to the fire?"

He slow-paced over to the table opposite her. "No. Do you?"

"There is a little moonlight. It will be cold later on."

He grunted, moved around toward her, felt for her fingers, and led her to the open doorway. Beyond, smoke-scent was strong. There was a sound of people up where the firelight showed brightly; in the opposite direction there was faint starshine and moonglow. He led her in that direction. They walked without speaking until a bony-tailed, slab-sided dog appeared, halted to watch them, and did not move nor make a sound as they went past. The handsome woman spoke. "I am worried, Henry."

He squeezed her fingers. "I told you—if they come, it'll be a while. We'll show them the graves, tell them the survivors left for Canada. They won't go after them because it will be too late."

She said, "No, not about Coffee Creek. About the gold."

He stopped and faced her. "As near as I can figure, Fawn, Amos and I know about it. You know because I told you. Sun Sister knows an' maybe she'll tell Dave Law. But no one knows where the vein is and except for me and Amos I doubt that anyone could find it. Ned took some pouches of it with him when he escaped the settlers down at Coffee Creek. The feller who killed him said he didn't have no pouches on him. Most likely he was lying, but whether he was or not don't matter a whole lot, because just about every place I ever been there's been stories of hidden gold mines, or lost ones, or abandoned ones. Lots of stories of treasure, which folks mostly don't believe. If this story gets out, maybe down at Bent's Siding, it's likely some fellers will come prospectin' up through here. We can tell them we heard of a gold vein somewhere east or west of the camp, fifty or so miles."

She stood in thought for a moment, then tugged at his hand. On their left was the creek, making its night-softened sounds. On their right was the Tenkiller cabin with its spread-eagled hides on the front wall. She did not even glance over there.

A burst of laughter reached them from back at the fire ring. She looked up at Henry. "I think the widow woman will stay. I heard her tell Amos it was beautiful up here."

"He will be happy."

"And Sun Sister too."

"Yes. Did you give her the money?"

"No. But I will . . . Not everyone will be happy."

He nodded his head, thinking of the graves.

"Henry?"

He looked around without speaking.

She looked sideways, smiling a little. "What do you want, Henry?"

"You. You and no more trouble. What do you want, Fawn?"

"You need a new hunting shirt. That one is getting thin. Some of the stains won't come out. I will make you one. You never ate right. I watched you. I used to think you would get sick through the winters."

He stopped and slowly turned. One thing he had learned long ago was that getting a direct answer from an Indian was about as easy as pulling teeth. He put both hands on her shoulders. "I'm waiting," he told her.

She did not slide out from under his touch. "We have two cabins."

He sighed under his breath. "I can put another room on mine. Two people need more than just one big room."

"I will help."

He continued to stand squarely in front of her, hands on her shoulders. "If you help me build the room the people will know."

She finally raised her eyes to his face. "Yes. That's how it used to be when I was a girl. The man and the woman just started doing things together, maybe making a house. Sometimes the old people were given horses, or guns, maybe hides. But neither one of us have any old people . . . I want to be your woman, Henry."

He pulled her close and held her, felt the full strength of her against him, was conscious of his own heartbeat, which was so strong he was sure she would notice it. If she did, she said nothing as she clung to him.

They stood like that for a long time. When they parted,

she looked up, flashing a white-toothed smile. "I feel like a girl, Henry."

He laughed at her. "You are a girl, Fawn."

Northward, the fire was dying; only a few people remained near it. Lights showed among the houses. At Amos's cabin the light was brightest. Henry thought he must have lit at least five candles. He idly thought of the widow's wagon down at Coffee Creek. They could take it apart and move it to the big meadow and reassemble it, but if she meant to stay he thought the best thing for her to do with her wagon would be to drive it over to Bent's Siding and sell it.

There was no road to the big meadow and there was no place to drive a big wagon up there, except around in circles.

Lauran Paine who, under his own name and various pseudonyms has written over 900 books, was born in Duluth, Minnesota, a descendant of the Revolutionary War patriot and author, Thomas Paine. His family moved to California when he was at an early age and his apprenticeship as a Western writer came about through the years he spent in the livestock trade, rodeos, and even motion pictures where he served as an extra because of his expert horsemanship in several films starring movie cowboy Johnny Mack Brown. In the late 1930s, Paine trapped wild horses in Northern Arizona and even, for a time, worked as a professional farrier. Paine came to know the Old West through the eyes of many who had been born in the previous century and he learned that Western life had been very different from the way it was portrayed on the screen. "I knew men who had killed other men," he later recalled. "But they were the exceptions. Prior to and during the Depression, people were just too busy eking out an existence to indulge in Saturday-night brawls." He served in the U.S. Navy in the Second World War and began writing for Western pulp magazines following his discharge. It is interesting to note that all of his earliest novels (written under his own name and the pseudonym Mark Carrel) were published in the British market and he soon had as strong a following in that country as in the United States. Paine's Western fiction is characterized by strong plots, authenticity, an apparently effortless ability to construct situation and character, and a preference for building his stories upon a solid foundation of historical fact. *Adobe Empire* (1956), one of his best novels, is a fictionalized account of the last twenty years in the life of trader William Bent and, in an off-trail way, has a melancholy, bittersweet texture that is not easily forgotten. *Moon Prairie* (1950), first published in the United States in 1994, is a memorable story set during the mountain man period of the frontier. In later novels such as *The Homesteaders* (1986) or *The Open Range Men* (1990), he showed that the special magic and power of his stories and characters had only matured along with his basic themes of changing times, changing attitudes, learning from experience, respecting nature, and the yearning for a simpler, more moderate way of life. His most recent Western novels include *Tears of the Heart*, *Lockwood* and *The White Bird*.